Favorite Fairy Tales

THE BROTHERS GRIMM

DOVER PUBLICATIONS, INC.
Mineola, New York

DOVER JUVENILE CLASSICS
EDITOR OF THIS VOLUME: JANET BAINE KOPITO

Bibliographical Note

This Dover edition, first published in 2001, is a new selection of unabridged tales from *Household Stories from the Collection of the Bros. Grimm,* translated by Lucy Crane, originally published by Macmillan and Company, New York, in 1886, except for the tales "Doctor Know-all," "The Seven Ravens," "The Lady and the Lion," "Jorinda and Joringel," and "The Twelve Dancing Princesses," which were originally published in *Grimm's Fairy Tales,* T. and A. Constable, Edinburgh, n.d. [1909].

Library of Congress Cataloging-in-Publication Data

Favorite fairy tales / The Brothers Grimm.
    p. cm. — (Dover juvenile classics)
    A selection of unabridged tales from Household stories from the collection of the Bros. Grimm, translated by Lucy Crane, originally published by Macmillan in 1886, and Grimm's fairy tales, originally published by T. and A. Constable in 1909.
    Summary: A collection of twenty-one traditional tales collected by the Grimm brothers.
    ISBN 0-486-41979-7 (pbk.)
    1. Fairy tales—Germany. [1. Fairy tales. 2. Folklore—Germany.] I. Grimm, Jacob, 1785–1863. II. Grimm, Wilhelm, 1786–1859. III. Title. IV. Series.

PZ8.G882 Fav 2001
398.2'0943—dc21

2001032403

Manufactured in the United States of America
Dover Publications, Inc., 31 East 2nd Street, Mineola, N.Y. 11501

Contents

Favorite Fairy Tales

Sleeping Beauty

IN TIMES PAST there lived a king and queen, who said to each other every day of their lives, "Would that we had a child!" and yet they had none. But it happened once that when the queen was bathing, there came a frog out of the water, and he squatted on the ground, and said to her,

"Thy wish shall be fulfilled; before a year has gone by, thou shalt bring a daughter into the world."

And as the frog foretold, so it happened; and the queen bore a daughter so beautiful that the king could not contain himself for joy, and he ordained a great feast. Not only did he bid to it his relations, friends, and acquaintances, but also the wise women, that they might be kind and favourable to the child. There were thirteen of them in his kingdom, but as he had only provided twelve golden plates for them to eat from, one of them had to be left out. However, the feast was celebrated with all splendour; and as it drew to an end, the wise women stood forward to present to the child their wonderful gifts: one bestowed virtue, one beauty, a third riches, and so on, whatever there is in the world to wish for. And when eleven of them had said their say, in came the uninvited thirteenth, burning to revenge herself, and without greeting or respect, she cried with a loud voice,

"In the fifteenth year of her age the princess shall prick herself with a spindle and shall fall down dead."

And without speaking one more word she turned away and left the hall. Every one was terrified at her saying, when the twelfth came forward, for she had not yet bestowed her gift, and though she could not do away with the evil prophecy, yet she could soften it, so she said,

"The princess shall not die, but fall into a deep sleep for a hundred years."

Now the king, being desirous of saving his child even from this misfortune, gave commandment that all the spindles in his kingdom should be burnt up.

The maiden grew up, adorned with all the gifts of the wise women; and she was so lovely, modest, sweet, and kind and clever, that no one who saw her could help loving her.

It happened one day, she being already fifteen years old, that the king and queen rode abroad, and the maiden was left behind alone in the castle. She wandered about into all the nooks and corners, and into all the chambers and parlours, as the fancy took her, till at last she came to an old tower. She climbed the narrow winding stair which led to a little door, with a rusty key sticking out of the lock; she turned the key, and the door opened, and there in the little room sat an old woman with a spindle, diligently spinning her flax.

"Good day, mother," said the princess, "what are you doing?"

"I am spinning," answered the old woman, nodding her head.

"What thing is that that twists round so briskly?" asked the maiden, and taking the spindle into her hand she began to spin; but no sooner had she touched it than the evil prophecy was fulfilled, and she pricked her finger with it. In that very moment she fell back upon the bed that stood there, and lay in a deep sleep. And this sleep fell upon the whole castle: the king and queen, who had returned and were in the great hall, fell fast asleep, and with them the whole court. The horses in their stalls, the dogs in the yard, the pigeons on the roof, the flies on the wall, the very fire that flickered on the hearth, became still, and slept like the rest; and the meat on the spit ceased roasting, and the cook, who was going to pull the scullion's hair for some mistake he had made, let him go, and went to sleep. And the wind ceased, and not a leaf fell from the trees about the castle.

Then round about that place there grew a hedge of thorns thicker every year, until at last the whole castle was hidden from view, and nothing of it could be seen but the vane on the roof. And a rumour went abroad in all that country of the beautiful sleeping Rosamond, for so was the princess called; and from time to time many kings' sons came and tried to force their way through the hedge; but it was impossible for them to do so, for the thorns held fast together like strong hands, and the young men were caught by them, and not being able to get free, there died a lamentable death.

Many a long year afterwards there came a king's son into that country, and heard an old man tell how there should be a castle standing behind the hedge of thorns, and that there a beautiful enchanted princess named Rosamond had slept for a hundred years, and with her the king and queen, and the whole court. The old man had been told by his grandfather that many king's sons had sought to pass the thorn-hedge, but had been caught and pierced by the thorns, and had died a miserable death. Then said the young man, "Nevertheless, I do not fear to try; I shall win through and see the lovely Rosamond." The good old man tried to dissuade him, but he would not listen to his words.

For now the hundred years were at an end, and the day had come when Rosamond should be awakened. When the prince drew near the hedge of thorns, it was changed into a hedge of beautiful large flowers, which parted and bent aside to let him pass, and then closed behind him in a thick hedge. When he reached the castle-yard, he saw the horses and brindled hunting-dogs lying asleep, and on the roof the pigeons were sitting with their heads under their wings. And when he came indoors, the flies on the wall were asleep, the cook in the kitchen had his hand uplifted to strike the scullion, and the kitchen-maid had the black fowl on her lap ready to pluck. Then he mounted higher, and saw in the hall the whole court lying asleep, and above them, on their thrones, slept the king and the queen. And still he went farther, and all was so quiet that he could hear his own breathing; and at last he came to the tower, and went up the winding stair, and opened the door of the little room where Rosamond lay. And when he saw her looking so lovely in her sleep, he could not turn away his eyes; and presently he stooped and kissed her, and she awaked, and opened her eyes, and looked very kindly on him. And she rose, and they went forth together, and the king and the queen and whole court waked up, and gazed on each other with great eyes of wonderment. And the horses in the yard got up and shook themselves, the hounds sprang up and wagged their tails, the pigeons on the roof drew their heads from under their wings, looked round, and flew into the field, the flies on the wall crept on a little farther, the kitchen fire leapt up and blazed, and cooked the meat, the joint on the spit began to roast, the cook gave the scullion such a box on the ear that he roared out, and the maid went on plucking the fowl.

Then the wedding of the prince and Rosamond was held with all splendour, and they lived very happily together until their lives' end.

The Golden Goose

THERE WAS a man who had three sons, the youngest of whom was called the Simpleton, and was despised, laughed at, and neglected, on every occasion. It happened one day that the eldest son wished to go into the forest to cut wood, and before he went his mother gave him a delicious pancake and a flask of wine, that he might not suffer from hunger or thirst. When he came into the forest a little old grey man met him, who wished him good day, and said,

"Give me a bit of cake out of your pocket, and let me have a drink of your wine; I am so hungry and thirsty."

But the prudent youth answered,

"Give you my cake and my wine? I haven't got any; be off with you."

And leaving the little man standing there, he went off. Then he began to fell a tree, but he had not been at it long before he made a wrong stroke, and the hatchet hit him in the arm, so that he was obliged to go home and get it bound up. That was what came of the little grey man.

Afterwards the second son went into the wood, and the mother gave to him, as to the eldest, a pancake and a flask of wine. The little old grey man met him also, and begged for a little bit of cake and a drink of wine. But the second son spoke out plainly, saying,

"What I give you I lose myself, so be off with you."

And leaving the little man standing there, he went off. The punishment followed; as he was chopping away at the tree, he hit himself in the leg so severely that he had to be carried home.

Then said the Simpleton,

"Father, let me go for once into the forest to cut wood"; and the father answered, "Your brothers have hurt themselves by so doing; give it up, you understand nothing about it."

But the Simpleton went on begging so long, that the father said at last,

"Well, be off with you; you will only learn by experience."

The mother gave him a cake (it was only made with water, and baked in the ashes), and with it a flask of sour beer. When he came into the forest the little old grey man met him, and greeted him saying,

"Give me a bit of your cake, and a drink from your flask; I am so hungry and thirsty."

And the Simpleton answered, "I have only a flour and water cake and sour beer; but if that is good enough for you, let us sit down together and eat." Then they sat down, and as the Simpleton took out his flour and water cake it became a rich pancake, and his sour beer became good wine; then they ate and drank, and afterwards the little man said,

"As you have such a kind heart, and share what you have so willingly, I will bestow good luck upon you. Yonder stands an old tree; cut it down, and at its roots you will find something," and thereupon the little man took his departure.

The Simpleton went there, and hewed away at the tree, and when it fell he saw, sitting among the roots, a goose with feathers of pure gold. He lifted it out and took it with him to an inn where he intended to stay the night. The landlord had three daughters who, when they saw the goose, were curious to know what wonderful kind of bird it was, and ended by longing for one of its golden feathers. The eldest thought, "I will wait for a good opportunity, and then I will pull out one of its feathers for myself"; and so, when the Simpleton was gone out, she seized the goose by its wing—but there her finger and hand had to stay, held fast. Soon after came the second sister with the same idea of plucking out one of the golden feathers for herself; but scarcely had she touched her sister, than she also was obliged to stay, held fast. Lastly came the third with the same intentions; but the others screamed out,

"Stay away! for heaven's sake stay away!"

But she did not see why she should stay away, and thought, "If they do so, why should not I?" and went towards them. But when she reached her sisters there she stopped, hanging on with them. And so they had to stay, all night. The next morning the Simpleton took the goose under his arm and went away, unmindful of the three girls that hung on to it. The three had always to run after him, left and right, wherever his legs carried him. In the midst of the fields they met the parson, who, when he saw the procession, said,

"Shame on you, girls, running after a young fellow through the fields like this," and forthwith he seized hold of the youngest by the hand to drag her away, but hardly had he touched her when he too was obliged to run after them himself. Not long after the sexton came that way, and seeing the respected parson following at the heels of the three girls, he called out,

"Ho, your reverence, whither away so quickly? You forget that we have another christening today"; and he seized hold of him by his gown; but no sooner had he touched him than he was obliged to follow on too. As the five tramped on, one after another, two peasants with their hoes came up from the fields, and the parson cried out to them, and begged them to come and set him and the sexton free, but no sooner had they touched the sexton than they had to follow on too; and now there were seven following the Simpleton and the goose.

By and by they came to a town where a king reigned, who had an only daughter who was so serious that no one could make her laugh; therefore the king had given out that whoever should make her laugh should have her in marriage. The Simpleton, when he heard this, went with his goose and his hangers-on into the presence of the king's daughter, and as soon as she saw the seven people following always one after the other, she burst out laughing, and seemed as if she could never stop. And so the Simpleton earned a right to her as his bride; but the king did not like him for a son-in-law and made all kinds of objections, and said he must first bring a man who could drink up a whole cellar of wine. The Simpleton thought that the little grey man would be able to help him, and went out into the forest, and there, on the very spot where he felled the tree, he saw a man sitting with a very sad countenance. The Simpleton asked him what was the matter, and he answered,

"I have a great thirst, which I cannot quench: cold water does not agree with me; I have indeed drunk up a whole cask of wine, but what good is a drop like that?"

Then said the Simpleton,

"I can help you; only come with me, and you shall have enough."

He took him straight to the king's cellar, and the man sat himself down before the big vats, and drank, and drank, and before a day was over he had drunk up the whole cellar-full. The Simpleton again asked for his bride, but the king was annoyed that a wretched fellow, called the Simpleton by everybody, should carry off his daughter, and so he made new conditions. He was to produce a man who could eat up a mountain of bread. The Simpleton did not hesitate long, but ran quickly off to the forest, and there in the same place sat a man who had fastened a strap round his body, making a very piteous face, and saying,

"I have eaten a whole bakehouse full of rolls, but what is the use of that when one is so hungry as I am? My stomach feels quite empty, and I am obliged to strap myself together, that I may not die of hunger."

The Simpleton was quite glad of this, and said,

"Get up quickly, and come along with me, and you shall have enough to eat."

He led him straight to the king's courtyard, where all the meal in the kingdom had been collected and baked into a mountain of bread. The man out of the forest settled himself down before it and hastened to eat, and in one day the whole mountain had disappeared.

Then the Simpleton asked for his bride the third time. The king, however, found one more excuse, and said he must have a ship that should be able to sail on land or on water.

"So soon," said he, "as you come sailing along with it, you shall have my daughter for your wife."

The Simpleton went straight to the forest, and there sat the little old grey man with whom he had shared his cake, and he said,

"I have eaten for you, and I have drunk for you, I will also give you the ship; and all because you were kind to me at the first."

Then he gave him the ship that could sail on land and on water, and when the king saw it he knew he could no longer withhold his daughter. The marriage took place immediately, and at the death of the king the Simpleton possessed the kingdom, and lived long and happily with his wife.

Hansel and Gretel

NEAR A GREAT forest there lived a poor woodcutter and his wife, and his two children; the boy's name was Hansel and the girl's Gretel. They had very little to bite or to sup, and once, when there was great dearth in the land, the man could not even gain the daily bread. As he lay in bed one night thinking of this, and turning and tossing, he sighed heavily, and said to his wife,

"What will become of us? we cannot even feed our children; there is nothing left for ourselves."

"I will tell you what, husband," answered the wife; "we will take the children early in the morning into the forest, where it is thickest; we will make them a fire, and we will give each of them a piece of bread, then we will go to our work and leave them alone; they will never find the way home again, and we shall be quit of them."

"No, wife," said the man, "I cannot do that; I cannot find in my heart to take my children into the forest and to leave them there alone; the wild animals would soon come and devour them."

"O you fool," said she, "then we will all four starve; you had better get the coffins ready,"—and she left him no peace until he consented.

"But I really pity the poor children," said the man.

The two children had not been able to sleep for hunger, and had heard what their step-mother had said to their father. Gretel wept bitterly, and said to Hansel,

"It is all over with us."

10

"Do be quiet, Gretel," said Hansel, "and do not fret; I will manage something." And when the parents had gone to sleep he got up, put on his little coat, opened the back door, and slipped out. The moon was shining brightly, and the white flints that lay in front of the house glistened like pieces of silver. Hansel stooped and filled the little pocket of his coat as full as it would hold. Then he went back again, and said to Gretel,

"Be easy, dear little sister, and go to sleep quietly; God will not forsake us," and laid himself down again in his bed.

When the day was breaking, and before the sun had risen, the wife came and awakened the two children, saying,

"Get up, you lazy bones; we are going into the forest to cut wood."

Then she gave each of them a piece of bread, and said,

"That is for dinner, and you must not eat it before then, for you will get no more."

Gretel carried the bread under her apron, for Hansel had his pockets full of the flints. Then they set off all together on their way to the forest. When they had gone a little way Hansel stood still and looked back towards the house, and this he did again and again, till his father said to him,

"Hansel, what are you looking at? take care not to forget your legs."

"O father," said Hansel, "I am looking at my little white kitten, who is sitting up on the roof to bid me good-bye."

"You young fool," said the woman, "that is not your kitten, but the sunshine on the chimney-pot."

Of course Hansel had not been looking at his kitten, but had been taking every now and then a flint from his pocket and dropping it on the road.

When they reached the middle of the forest the father told the children to collect wood to make a fire to keep them warm; and Hansel and Gretel gathered brushwood enough for a little mountain; and it was set on fire, and when the flame was burning quite high the wife said,

"Now lie down by the fire and rest yourselves, you children, and we will go and cut wood; and when we are ready we will come and fetch you."

So Hansel and Gretel sat by the fire, and at noon they each ate their pieces of bread. They thought their father was in the wood all the time, as they seemed to hear the strokes of the axe: but really it was only a dry branch hanging to a withered tree that the wind moved to and fro. So when they had stayed there a long time their eyelids closed with weariness, and they fell fast asleep. When at last they woke it was night, and Gretel began to cry, and said,

"How shall we ever get out of this wood?" But Hansel comforted her, saying,

"Wait a little while longer, until the moon rises, and then we can easily find the way home."

And when the full moon got up Hansel took his little sister by the hand, and followed the way where the flint stones shone like silver, and showed them the road. They walked on the whole night through, and at the break of day they came to their father's house. They knocked at the door, and when the wife opened it and saw that it was Hansel and Gretel she said,

"You naughty children, why did you sleep so long in the wood? we thought you were never coming home again!"

But the father was glad, for it had gone to his heart to leave them both in the woods alone.

Not very long after that there was again great scarcity in those parts, and the children heard their mother say at night in bed to their father,

"Everything is finished up; we have only half a loaf, and after that the tale comes to an end. The children must be off; we will take them farther into the wood this time, so that they shall not be able to find the way back again; there is no other way to manage."

The man felt sad at heart, and he thought,

"It would be better to share one's last morsel with one's children."

But the wife would listen to nothing that he said, but

scolded and reproached him. He who says A must say B too, and when a man has given in once he has to do it a second time.

But the children were not asleep, and had heard all the talk. When the parents had gone to sleep Hansel got up to go out and get more flint stones, as he did before, but the wife had locked the door, and Hansel could not get out; but he comforted his little sister, and said,

"Don't cry, Gretel, and go to sleep quietly, and God will help us."

Early the next morning the wife came and pulled the children out of bed. She gave them each a little piece of bread—less than before; and on the way to the wood Hansel crumbled the bread in his pocket, and often stopped to throw a crumb on the ground.

"Hansel, what are you stopping behind and staring for?" said the father.

"I am looking at my little pigeon sitting on the roof, to say good-bye to me," answered Hansel.

"You fool," said the wife, "that is no pigeon, but the morning sun shining on the chimney-pot."

Hansel went on as before, and strewed bread crumbs all along the road.

The woman led the children far into the wood, where they had never been before in all their lives. And again there was a large fire made, and the mother said,

"Sit still there, you children, and when you are tired you can go to sleep; we are going into the forest to cut wood, and in the evening, when we are ready to go home, we will come and fetch you."

So when noon came Gretel shared her bread with Hansel, who had strewed his along the road. Then they went to sleep, and the evening passed, and no one came for the poor children. When they awoke it was dark night, and Hansel comforted his little sister, and said,

"Wait a little, Gretel, until the moon gets up, then we shall be able to see the way home by the crumbs of bread that I have scattered along it."

So when the moon rose they got up, but they could find
no crumbs of bread, for the birds of the woods and of the
fields had come and picked them up. Hansel thought they
might find the way all the same, but they could not. They
went on all that night, and the next day from the morning
until the evening, but they could not find the way out of
the wood, and they were very hungry, for they had nothing to eat but the few berries they could pick up. And
when they were so tired that they could no longer drag
themselves along, they lay down under a tree and fell
asleep.

It was now the third morning since they had left their
father's house. They were always trying to get back to it,
but instead of that they only found themselves farther in
the wood, and if help had not soon come they would have
been starved. About noon they saw a pretty snow-white
bird sitting on a bough, and singing so sweetly that they
stopped to listen. And when he had finished the bird
spread his wings and flew before them, and they followed
after him until they came to a little house, and the bird
perched on the roof, and when they came nearer they saw
that the house was built of bread, and roofed with cakes;
and the window was of transparent sugar.

"We will have some of this," said Hansel, "and make a
fine meal. I will eat a piece of the roof, Gretel, and you can
have some of the window—that will taste sweet."

So Hansel reached up and broke off a bit of the roof, just
to see how it tasted, and Gretel stood by the window and
gnawed at it. Then they heard a thin voice call out from
inside,

> "Nibble, nibble, like a mouse,
> Who is nibbling at my house?"

And the children answered,

> "Never mind,
> It is the wind."

And they went on eating, never disturbing themselves. Hansel, who found that the roof tasted very nice, took down a great piece of it, and Gretel pulled out a large round window-pane, and sat her down and began upon it. Then the door opened, and an aged woman came out, leaning upon a crutch. Hansel and Gretel felt very frightened, and let fall what they had in their hands. The old woman, however, nodded her head, and said,

"Ah, my dear children, how come you here? you must come indoors and stay with me, you will be no trouble."

So she took them each by the hand, and led them into her little house. And there they found a good meal laid out, of milk and pancakes, with sugar, apples, and nuts. After that she showed them two little white beds, and Hansel and Gretel laid themselves down on them, and thought they were in heaven.

The old woman, although her behaviour was so kind, was a wicked witch, who lay in wait for children, and had built the little house on purpose to entice them. When they were once inside she used to kill them, cook them, and eat them, and then it was a feast-day with her. The witch's eyes were red, and she could not see very far, but she had a keen scent, like the beasts, and knew very well when human creatures were near. When she knew that Hansel and Gretel were coming, she gave a spiteful laugh, and said triumphantly,

"I have them, and they shall not escape me!"

Early in the morning, before the children were awake, she got up to look at them, and as they lay sleeping so peacefully with round rosy cheeks, she said to herself,

"What a fine feast I shall have!"

Then she grasped Hansel with her withered hand, and led him into a little stable, and shut him up behind a grating; and call and scream as he might, it was no good. Then she went back to Gretel and shook her, crying,

"Get up, lazy bones; fetch water, and cook something nice for your brother; he is outside in the stable, and must be fattened up. And when he is fat enough I will eat him."

Gretel began to weep bitterly, but it was of no use, she had to do what the wicked witch bade her.

And so the best kind of victuals was cooked for poor Hansel, while Gretel got nothing but crab-shells. Each morning the old woman visited the little stable, and cried,

"Hansel, stretch out your finger, that I may tell if you will soon be fat enough."

Hansel, however, used to hold out a little bone, and the old woman, who had weak eyes, could not see what it was, and supposing it to be Hansel's finger, wondered very much that it was not getting fatter. When four weeks had passed and Hansel seemed to remain so thin, she lost patience and could wait no longer.

"Now then, Gretel," cried she to the little girl; "be quick and draw water; be Hansel fat or be he lean, to-morrow I must kill and cook him."

Oh what a grief for the poor little sister to have to fetch water, and how the tears flowed down over her cheeks!

"Dear God, pray help us!" cried she; "if we had been devoured by wild beasts in the wood at least we should have died together."

"Spare me your lamentations," said the old woman; "they are of no avail."

Early next morning Gretel had to get up, make the fire, and fill the kettle.

"First we will do the baking," said the old woman; "I have heated the oven already, and kneaded the dough."

She pushed poor Gretel towards the oven, out of which the flames were already shining.

"Creep in," said the witch, "and see if it is properly hot, so that the bread may be baked."

And Gretel once in, she meant to shut the door upon her and let her be baked, and then she would have eaten her. But Gretel perceived her intention, and said,

"I don't know how to do it: how shall I get in?"

"Stupid goose," said the old woman, "the opening is big enough, do you see? I could get in myself!" and she stooped down and put her head in the oven's mouth.

Then Gretel gave her a push, so that she went in farther, and she shut the iron door upon her, and put up the bar. Oh how frightfully she howled! but Gretel ran away, and left the wicked witch to burn miserably. Gretel went straight to Hansel, opened the stable-door, and cried,

"Hansel, we are free! the old witch is dead!"

Then out flew Hansel like a bird from its cage as soon as the door is opened. How rejoiced they both were! how they fell each on the other's neck! and danced about, and kissed each other! And as they had nothing more to fear they went over all the old witch's house, and in every corner there stood chests of pearls and precious stones.

"This is something better than flint stones," said Hansel, as he filled his pockets, and Gretel, thinking she also would like to carry something home with her, filled her apron full.

"Now, away we go," said Hansel;—"if we only can get out of the witch's wood."

When they had journeyed a few hours they came to a great piece of water.

"We can never get across this," said Hansel, "I see no stepping-stones and no bridge."

"And there is no boat either," said Gretel; "but here comes a white duck; if I ask her she will help us over." So she cried,

> "Duck, duck, here we stand,
>   Hansel and Gretel, on the land,
>   Stepping-stones and bridge we lack,
>   Carry us over on your nice white back."

And the duck came accordingly, and Hansel got upon her and told his sister to come too.

"No," answered Gretel, "that would be too hard upon the duck; we can go separately, one after the other."

And that was how it was managed, and after that they went on happily, until they came to the wood, and the way grew more and more familiar, till at last they saw in the distance their father's house. Then they ran till they came up to it, rushed in at the door, and fell on their father's neck. The man had not had a quiet hour since he left his children in the wood; but the wife was dead. And when Gretel opened her apron the pearls and precious stones were scattered all over the room, and Hansel took one handful after another out of his pocket. Then was all care at an end, and they lived in great joy together.

The Bremen Town Musicians

THERE WAS ONCE an ass whose master had made him carry sacks to the mill for many a long year, but whose strength began at last to fail, so that each day as it came found him less capable of work. Then his master began to think of turning him out, but the ass, guessing that something was in the wind that boded him no good, ran away, taking the road to Bremen; for there he thought he might get an engagement as town musician. When he had gone a little way he found a hound lying by the side of the road panting, as if he had run a long way.

"Now, Holdfast, what are you so out of breath about?" said the ass.

"Oh dear!" said the dog, "now I am old, I get weaker every day, and can do no good in the hunt, so, as my master was going to have me killed, I have made my escape; but now, how am I to gain a living?"

"I will tell you what," said the ass, "I am going to Bremen to become town musician. You may as well go with me, and take up music too. I can play the lute, and you can beat the drum."

And the dog consented, and they walked on together. It was not long before they came to a cat sitting in the road, looking as dismal as three wet days.

"Now then, what is the matter with you, old shaver?" said the ass.

"I should like to know who would be cheerful when his neck is in danger," answered the cat. "Now that I am old

19

my teeth are getting blunt, and I would rather sit by the oven and purr than run about after mice, and my mistress wanted to drown me; so I took myself off; but good advice is scarce, and I do not know what is to become of me."

"Go with us to Bremen," said the ass, "and become town musician. You understand serenading."

The cat thought well of the idea, and went with them accordingly. After that the three travellers passed by a yard, and a cock was perched on the gate crowing with all his might.

"Your cries are enough to pierce bone and marrow," said the ass; "what is the matter?"

"I have foretold good weather for Lady-day, so that all the shirts may be washed and dried; and now on Sunday morning company is coming, and the mistress has told the cook that I must be made into soup, and this evening my neck is to be wrung, so that I am crowing with all my might while I can."

"You had much better go with us, Chanticleer," said the ass. "We are going to Bremen. At any rate that will be better than dying. You have a powerful voice, and when we are all performing together it will have a very good effect."

So the cock consented, and they went on all four together.

But Bremen was too far off to be reached in one day, and towards evening they came to a wood, where they determined to pass the night. The ass and the dog lay down under a large tree; the cat got up among the branches, and the cock flew up to the top, as that was the safest place for him. Before he went to sleep he looked all round him to the four points of the compass, and perceived in the distance a little light shining, and he called out to his companions that there must be a house not far off, as he could see a light, so the ass said,

"We had better get up and go there, for these are uncomfortable quarters." The dog began to fancy a few bones, not quite bare, would do him good. And they all set off in the direction of the light, and it grew larger and brighter, until at last it led them to a robber's house, all lighted up. The ass, being the biggest, went up to the window, and looked in.

"Well, what do you see?" asked the dog.

"What do I see?" answered the ass; "here is a table set out with splendid eatables and drinkables, and robbers sitting at it and making themselves very comfortable."

"That would just suit us," said the cock.

"Yes, indeed, I wish we were there," said the ass. Then they consulted together how it should be managed so as to get the robbers out of the house, and at last they hit on a plan. The ass was to place his forefeet on the window-sill, the dog was to get on the ass's back, the cat on the top of the dog, and lastly the cock was to fly up and perch on the cat's head. When that was done, at a given signal they all began to perform their music. The ass brayed, the dog barked, the cat mewed, and the cock crowed; then they burst through into the room, breaking all the panes of glass. The robbers fled at the dreadful sound; they thought it was some goblin, and fled to the wood in the utmost terror. Then the four companions sat down to table, made free with the remains of the meal, and feasted as if they had been hungry for a month. And when they had finished they put out the lights, and each sought out a sleeping-place to suit his nature and habits. The ass laid himself down outside on the dunghill, the dog behind the door, the cat on the hearth by the warm ashes, and the cock settled himself in the cockloft, and as they were all tired with their long journey they soon fell fast asleep.

When midnight drew near, and the robbers from afar saw that no light was burning, and that everything appeared quiet, their captain said to them that he thought that they had run away without reason, telling one of them to go and reconnoitre. So one of them went, and found everything quite quiet; he went into the kitchen to strike a light, and taking the glowing fiery eyes of the cat for burning coals, he held a match to them in order to kindle it. But the cat, not seeing the joke, flew into his face, spitting and scratching. Then he cried out in terror, and ran to get out at the back door, but the dog, who was lying there, ran at him and bit his leg; and as he was rushing through the yard by the dunghill the ass struck out and gave him a great kick with his hindfoot; and the cock, who had been wakened with the noise, and felt quite brisk, cried out, "Cock-a-doodle-doo!"

Then the robber got back as well as he could to his captain, and said, "Oh dear! in that house there is a grewsome witch, and I felt her breath and her long nails in my face; and by the door there stands a man who stabbed me in the leg with a knife; and in the yard there lies a black spectre, who beat me with his wooden club; and above, upon the roof, there sits the justice, who cried, 'Bring that rogue here!' And so I ran away from the place as fast as I could."

From that time forward the robbers never ventured to that house, and the four Bremen town musicians found themselves so well off where they were, that there they stayed. And the person who last related this tale is still living, as you see.

The Golden Bird

I N TIMES GONE by there was a king who had at the back of his castle a beautiful pleasure-garden, in which stood a tree that bore golden apples. As the apples ripened they were counted, but one morning one was missing. Then the king was angry, and he ordered that watch should be kept about the tree every night. Now the king had three sons, and he sent the eldest to spend the whole night in the garden; so he watched till midnight, and then he could keep off sleep no longer, and in the morning another apple was missing. The second son had to watch the following night; but it fared no better, for when twelve o'clock had struck he went to sleep, and in the morning another apple was missing. Now came the turn of the third son to watch, and he was ready to do so; but the king had less trust in him, and believed he would acquit himself still worse than his brothers, but in the end he consented to let him try. So the young man lay down under the tree to watch, and resolved that sleep should not be master. When it struck twelve something came rushing through the air, and he saw in the moonlight a bird flying towards him, whose feathers glittered like gold. The bird perched upon the tree, and had already pecked off an apple, when the young man let fly an arrow at it. The bird flew away, but the arrow had struck its plumage, and one of its golden feathers fell to the ground; the young man picked it up, and taking it next morning to the king, told him what had happened in the night. The king called his council together, and all declared that such a feather was worth more than the whole kingdom.

"Since the feather is so valuable," said the king, "one is not enough for me; I must and will have the whole bird."

So the eldest son set off, and relying on his own cleverness he thought he should soon find the golden bird. When he had gone some distance he saw a fox sitting at the edge of a wood, and he pointed his gun at him. The fox cried out,

"Do not shoot me, and I will give you good counsel. You are on your way to find the golden bird, and this evening you will come to a village, in which two taverns stand facing each other. One will be brightly lighted up, and there will be plenty of merriment going on inside; do not mind about that, but go into the other one, although it will look to you very uninviting."

"How can a silly beast give one any rational advice?" thought the king's son, and let fly at the fox, but missed him, and he stretched out his tail and ran quick into the wood. Then the young man went on his way, and towards evening he came to the village, and there stood the two taverns; in one singing and dancing was going on, the other looked quite dull and wretched. "I should be a fool," said he, "to go into that dismal place, while there is anything so good close by." So he went into the merry inn, and there lived in clover, quite forgetting the bird and his father, and all good counsel.

As time went on, and the eldest son never came home, the second son set out to seek the golden bird. He met with the fox, just as the eldest did, and received good advice from him without attending to it. And when he came to the two taverns, his brother was standing and calling to him at the window of one of them, out of which came sounds of merriment; so he could not resist, but went in and revelled to his heart's content.

And then, as time went on, the youngest son wished to go forth, and to try his luck, but his father would not consent.

"It would be useless," said he; "he is much less likely to find the bird than his brothers, and if any misfortune were to happen to him he would not know how to help himself; his wits are none of the best."

But at last, as there was no peace to be had, he let him go. By the side of the wood sat the fox, begged him to spare his life, and gave him good counsel. The young man was kind, and said,

"Be easy, little fox, I will do you no harm."

"You shall not repent of it," answered the fox, "and that you may get there all the sooner, get up and sit on my tail."

And no sooner had he done so than the fox began to run, and off they went over stock and stone, so that the wind whistled in their hair. When they reached the village the young man got down, and, following the fox's advice, went into the mean-looking tavern, without hesitating, and there he passed a quiet night. The next morning, when he went out into the field, the fox, who was sitting there already, said,

"I will tell you further what you have to do. Go straight on until you come to a castle, before which a great band of soldiers lie, but do not trouble yourself about them, for they will be all asleep and snoring; pass through them and forward into the castle, and go through all the rooms, until you come to one where there is a golden bird hanging in a wooden cage. Near at hand will stand empty a golden cage of state, but you must beware of taking the bird out of his ugly cage and putting him into the fine one; if you do so you will come to harm."

After he had finished saying this the fox stretched out his tail again, and the king's son sat him down upon it; then away they went over stock and stone, so that the wind whistled through their hair. And when the king's son reached the castle he found everything as the fox had said: and he at last entered the room where the golden bird was hanging in a wooden cage, while a golden one was standing by; the three golden apples too were in the room. Then, thinking it foolish to let the beautiful bird stay in that mean and ugly cage, he opened the door of it, took hold of it, and put it in the golden one. In the same moment the bird uttered a piercing cry. The soldiers awaked, rushed in, seized the king's son and put him in prison. The next morning he was brought before a judge, and, as he confessed everything, condemned to death. But the king said he would spare his life on one condition, that he should bring him the golden horse whose paces were swifter than the wind, and that then he should also receive the golden bird as a reward.

So the king's son set off to find the golden horse, but he sighed, and was very sad, for how should it be accomplished? And then he saw his old friend the fox sitting by the roadside.

"Now, you see," said the fox, "all this has happened, because you would not listen to me. But be of good courage, I will bring you through, and will tell you how you are to get the golden horse. You must go straight on until you come to a castle, where the horse stands in his stable; before the stable-door the grooms will be lying, but they will all be asleep and snoring; and you can go and quietly lead out the horse. But one thing you must mind— take care to put upon him the plain saddle of wood and leather, and not the golden one, which will hang close by; otherwise it will go badly with you."

Then the fox stretched out his tail, and the king's son seated himself upon it, and away they went over stock and stone until the wind whistled through their hair. And everything happened just as the fox had said, and he came to the stall where the golden horse was: and as he was about to put on him the plain saddle, he thought to himself,

"Such a beautiful animal would be disgraced were I not to put on him the good saddle, which becomes him so well." However, no sooner did the horse feel the golden saddle touch him than he began to neigh. And the grooms all awoke, seized the king's son and threw him into prison.

The next morning he was delivered up to justice and condemned to death, but the king promised him his life, and
also to bestow upon him the golden horse, if he could
convey thither the beautiful princess of the golden castle.

With a heavy heart the king's son set out, but by great
good luck he soon met with the faithful fox.

"I ought now to leave you to your own ill-luck," said the
fox, "but I am sorry for you, and will once more help you
in your need. Your way lies straight up to the golden castle: you will arrive there in the evening, and at night, when
all is quiet, the beautiful princess goes to the bath. And as
she is entering the bathing-house, go up to her and give
her a kiss, then she will follow you, and you can lead her
away; but do not suffer her first to go and take leave of her
parents, or it will go ill with you."

Then the fox stretched out his tail; the king's son seated
himself upon it, and away they went over stock and stone,
so that the wind whistled through their hair. And when he
came to the golden castle all was as the fox had said. He
waited until midnight, when all lay in deep sleep, and then
as the beautiful princess went to the bathing-house he
went up to her and gave her a kiss, and she willingly
promised to go with him, but she begged him earnestly,
and with tears, that he would let her first go and take
leave of her parents. At first he denied her prayer, but as
she wept so much the more, and fell at his feet, he gave in
at last. And no sooner had the princess reached her
father's bedside than he, and all who were in the castle,
waked up, and the young man was seized and thrown into
prison.

The next morning the king said to him,

"Thy life is forfeit, but thou shalt find grace if thou canst
level that mountain that lies before my windows, and over
which I am not able to see: and if this is done within eight
days thou shalt have my daughter for a reward."

So the king's son set to work, and dug and shovelled
away without ceasing, but when, on the seventh day, he
saw how little he had accomplished, and that all his work

was as nothing, he fell into great sadness, and gave up all hope. But on the evening of the seventh day the fox appeared, and said,

"You do not deserve that I should help you, but go now and lie down to sleep, and I will do the work for you."

The next morning when he awoke, and looked out of the window, the mountain had disappeared. The young man hastened full of joy to the king, and told him that his behest was fulfilled, and, whether the king liked it or not, he had to keep his word, and let his daughter go.

So they both went away together, and it was not long before the faithful fox came up to them.

"Well, you have got the best first," said he; "but you must know the golden horse belongs to the princess of the golden castle."

"But how shall I get it?" asked the young man.

"I am going to tell you," answered the fox. "First, go to the king who sent you to the golden castle, and take to him the beautiful princess. There will then be very great rejoicing; he will willingly give you the golden horse, and they will lead him out to you; then mount him without delay, and stretch out your hand to each of them to take leave, and last of all to the princess, and when you have her by the hand swing her up on the horse behind you, and off you go! Nobody will be able to overtake you, for that horse goes swifter than the wind."

And so it was all happily done, and the king's son carried off the beautiful princess on the golden horse. The fox did not stay behind, and he said to the young man,

"Now, I will help you to get the golden bird. When you draw near the castle where the bird is, let the lady alight, and I will take her under my care; then you must ride the golden horse into the castle-yard, and there will be great rejoicing to see it, and they will bring out to you the golden bird; as soon as you have the cage in your hand, you must start off back to us, and then you shall carry the lady away."

The plan was successfully carried out; and when the young man returned with the treasure, the fox said,

"Now, what will you give me for my reward?"

"What would you like?" asked the young man.

"When we are passing through the wood, I desire that you should slay me, and cut my head and feet off."

"That were a strange sign of gratitude," said the king's son, "and I could not possibly do such a thing."

Then said the fox,

"If you will not do it, I must leave you; but before I go let me give you some good advice. Beware of two things: buy no gallows-meat, and sit at no brook-side." With that the fox ran off into the wood.

The young man thought to himself, "That is a wonderful animal, with most singular ideas. How should any one buy gallows-meat? and I am sure I have no particular fancy for sitting by a brook-side."

So he rode on with the beautiful princess, and their way led them through the village where his two brothers had stayed. There they heard great outcry and noise, and when he asked what it was all about, they told him that two people were going to be hanged. And when he drew near he saw that it was his two brothers, who had done all sorts of evil tricks, and had wasted all their goods. He asked if there were no means of setting them free.

"Oh yes! if you will buy them off," answered the people; "but why should you spend your money in redeeming such worthless men?"

But he persisted in doing so; and when they were let go they all went on their journey together.

After a while they came to the wood where the fox had met them first, and there it seemed so cool and sheltered from the sun's burning rays that the two brothers said,

"Let us rest here for a little by the brook, and eat and drink to refresh ourselves."

The young man consented, quite forgetting the fox's warning, and he seated himself by the brook-side, suspecting no evil. But the two brothers thrust him backwards into the brook, seized the princess, the horse, and the bird, and went home to their father.

"Is not this the golden bird that we bring?" said they; "and we have also the golden horse, and the princess of the golden castle."

Then there was great rejoicing in the royal castle, but the horse did not feed, the bird did not chirp, and the princess sat still and wept.

The youngest brother, however, had not perished. The brook was, by good fortune, dry, and he fell on soft moss without receiving any hurt, but he could not get up again. But in his need the faithful fox was not lacking; he came up running, and reproached him for having forgotten his advice.

"But I cannot forsake you all the same," said he; "I will help you back again into daylight." So he told the young man to grasp his tail, and hold on to it fast, and so he drew him up again.

"Still you are not quite out of all danger," said the fox; "your brothers, not being certain of your death, have surrounded the wood with sentinels, who are to put you to death if you let yourself be seen."

A poor beggar-man was sitting by the path, and the young man changed clothes with him, and went clad in that wise into the king's courtyard. Nobody knew him, but the bird began to chirp, and the horse began to feed, and the beautiful princess ceased weeping.

"What does this mean?" said the king, astonished.

The princess answered.

"I cannot tell, except that I was sad, and now I am joyful; it is to me as if my rightful bridegroom had returned."

Then she told him all that happened, although the two brothers had threatened to put her to death if she let out anything. The king then ordered every person who was in the castle to be brought before him, and with the rest came the young man like a beggar in his wretched garments; but the princess knew him, and greeted him well, falling on his neck and kissing him. The wicked brothers were seized and put to death, and the youngest brother was married to the princess, and succeeded to the inheritance of his father.

But what became of the poor fox? Long afterwards the king's son was going through the wood, and the fox met him and said,

"Now you have everything that you can wish for, but my misfortunes never come to an end, and it lies in your power to free me from them." And once more he prayed the king's son earnestly to slay him, and cut off his head and feet. So, at last, he consented, and no sooner was it done than the fox was changed into a man, and was no other than the brother of the beautiful princess; and thus he was set free from a spell that had bound him for a long, long time.

And now, indeed, there lacked nothing to their happiness as long as they lived.

The Frog Prince

IN THE OLD times, when it was still of some use to wish for the thing one wanted, there lived a King whose daughters were all handsome, but the youngest was so beautiful that the sun himself, who has seen so much, wondered each time he shone over her because of her beauty. Near the royal castle there was a great dark wood, and in the wood under an old linden-tree was a well; and when the day was hot, the King's daughter used to go forth into the wood and sit by the brink of the cool well, and if the time seemed long, she would take out a golden ball, and throw it up and catch it again, and this was her favourite pastime.

Now it happened one day that the golden ball, instead of falling back into the maiden's little hand which had sent it aloft, dropped to the ground near the edge of the well and rolled in. The King's daughter followed it with her eyes as it sank, but the well was deep, so deep that the bottom could not be seen. Then she began to weep, and she wept and wept as if she could never be comforted. And in the midst of her weeping she heard a voice saying to her,

"What ails thee, King's daughter? thy tears would melt a heart of stone."

And when she looked to see where the voice came from, there was nothing but a frog stretching his thick ugly head out of the water.

"Oh, is it you, old waddler?" said she; "I weep because my golden ball has fallen into the well."

"Never mind, do not weep," answered the frog; "I can help you; but what will you give me if I fetch up your ball again?"

"Whatever you like, dear frog," said she; "any of my clothes, my pearls and jewels, or even the golden crown that I wear."

"Thy clothes, thy pearls and jewels, and thy golden crown are not for me," answered the frog; "but if thou wouldst love me, and have me for thy companion and play-fellow, and let me sit by thee at table, and eat from thy plate, and drink from thy cup, and sleep in thy little bed,—if thou wouldst promise all this, then would I dive below the water and fetch thee thy golden ball again."

"Oh yes," she answered; "I will promise it all, whatever you want, if you will only get me my ball again."

But she thought to herself, "What nonsense he talks! as if he could do anything but sit in the water and croak with the other frogs, or could possibly be any one's companion."

But the frog, as soon as he heard her promise, drew his head under the water and sank down out of sight, but after a while he came to the surface again with the ball in his mouth, and he threw it on the grass.

The King's daughter was overjoyed to see her pretty plaything again, and she caught it up and ran off with it.

"Stop, stop!" cried the frog; "take me up too; I cannot run as fast as you!"

But it was of no use, for croak, croak after her as he might, she would not listen to him, but made haste home, and very soon forgot all about the poor frog, who had to betake himself to his well again.

The next day, when the King's daughter was sitting at table with the King and all the court, and eating from her golden plate, there came something pitter patter up the marble stairs, and then there came a knocking at the door, and a voice crying "Youngest King's daughter, let me in!"

And she got up and ran to see who it could be, but when she opened the door, there was the frog sitting outside.

Then she shut the door hastily and went back to her seat, feeling very uneasy. The King noticed how quickly her heart was beating, and said,

"My child, what are you afraid of? is there a giant standing at the door ready to carry you away?"

"Oh no," answered she; "no giant, but a horrid frog."

"And what does the frog want?" asked the King.

"O dear father," answered she, "when I was sitting by the well yesterday, and playing with my golden ball, it fell into the water, and while I was crying for the loss of it, the frog came and got it again for me on condition I would let him be my companion, but I never thought that he could leave the water and come after me; but now there he is outside the door, and he wants to come in to me."

And then they all heard him knocking the second time and crying,

> "Youngest King's daughter,
>   Open to me!
> By the well water
> What promised you me?
> Youngest King's daughter,
>   Now open to me!"

"That which thou hast promised must thou perform," said the King; "so go now and let him in."

So she went and opened the door, and the frog hopped in, following at her heels, till she reached her chair. Then he stopped and cried,

"Lift me up to sit by you."

But she delayed doing so until the King ordered her. When once the frog was on the chair, he wanted to get on the table, and there he sat and said,

"Now push your golden plate a little nearer, so that we may eat together."

And so she did, but everybody might see how unwilling she was, and the frog feasted heartily, but every morsel seemed to stick in her throat.

"I have had enough now," said the frog at last, "and as I am tired, you must carry me to your room, and make ready your silken bed, and we will lie down and go to sleep."

Then the King's daughter began to weep, and was afraid of the cold frog, that nothing would satisfy him but he must sleep in her pretty clean bed. Now the King grew angry with her, saying,

"That which thou hast promised in thy time of necessity, must thou now perform."

So she picked up the frog with her finger and thumb, carried him upstairs and put him in a corner, and when she had lain down to sleep, he came creeping up, saying, "I am tired and want sleep as much as you; take me up, or I will tell your father."

Then she felt beside herself with rage, and picking him up, she threw him with all her strength against the wall, crying,

"Now will you be quiet, you horrid frog!"

But as he fell, he ceased to be a frog, and became all at once a prince with beautiful kind eyes. And it came to pass that, with her father's consent, they became bride and bridegroom. And he told her how a wicked witch had bound him by her spells, and how no one but she alone could have released him, and that they two would go together to his father's kingdom. And there came to the door a carriage drawn by eight white horses, with white plumes on their heads, and with golden harness, and behind the carriage was standing faithful Henry, the servant of the young prince. Now, faithful Henry had suffered such care and pain when his master was turned into a frog, that he had been obliged to wear three iron bands over his heart, to keep it from breaking with trouble and anxiety. When the carriage started to take the prince to his kingdom, and faithful Henry had helped them both in, he got up behind, and was full of joy at his master's deliverance. And when they had gone a part of the way, the prince heard a sound at the back of the carriage, as if something had broken, and he turned round and cried,

"Henry, the wheel must be breaking!" but Henry answered,

> "The wheel does not break,
> 'Tis the band round my heart
> That, to lessen its ache,
> When I grieved for your sake,
> I bound round my heart."

Again, and yet once again there was the same sound, and the prince thought it must be the wheel breaking, but it was the breaking of the other bands from faithful Henry's heart, because it was now so relieved and happy.

Rumpelstiltskin

THERE WAS ONCE a miller who was poor, but he had one beautiful daughter. It happened one day that he came to speak with the king, and, to give himself consequence, he told him that he had a daughter who could spin gold out of straw. The king said to the miller,

"That is an art that pleases me well; if thy daughter is as clever as you say, bring her to my castle to-morrow, that I may put her to the proof."

When the girl was brought to him, he led her into a room that was quite full of straw, and gave her a wheel and spindle, and said,

"Now set to work, and if by the early morning thou hast not spun this straw to gold thou shalt die." And he shut the door himself, and left her there alone.

And so the poor miller's daughter was left there sitting, and could not think what to do for her life; she had no notion how to set to work to spin gold from straw, and her distress grew so great that she began to weep. Then all at once the door opened, and in came a little man, who said,

"Good evening, miller's daughter; why are you crying?"

"Oh!" answered the girl, "I have got to spin gold out of straw, and I don't understand the business."

Then the little man said,

"What will you give me if I spin it for you?"

"My necklace," said the girl.

The little man took the necklace, seated himself before the wheel, and whirr, whirr, whirr! three times round and the bobbin was full; then he took up another, and whirr, whirr, whirr! three times round, and that was full; and so he went on till the morning, when all the straw had been spun, and all the bobbins were full of gold. At sunrise came the king, and when he saw the gold he was astonished and very much rejoiced, for he was very avaricious. He had the miller's daughter taken into another room filled with straw, much bigger than the last, and told her that as she valued her life she must spin it all in one night. The girl did not know what to do, so she began to cry, and then the door opened, and the little man appeared and said,

"What will you give me if I spin all this straw into gold?"

"The ring from my finger," answered the girl.

So the little man took the ring, and began again to send the wheel whirring round, and by the next morning all the straw was spun into glistening gold. The king was rejoiced beyond measure at the sight, but as he could never have enough of gold, he had the miller's daughter taken into a still larger room full of straw, and said,

"This, too, must be spun in one night, and if you accomplish it, you shall be my wife." For he thought, "Although she is but a miller's daughter, I am not likely to find any one richer in the whole world."

As soon as the girl was left alone, the little man appeared for the third time and said,

"What will you give me if I spin the straw for you this time?"

"I have nothing left to give," answered the girl.

"Then you must promise me the first child you have after you are queen," said the little man.

"But who knows whether that will happen?" thought the girl; but as she did not know what else to do in her necessity, she promised the little man what he desired, upon which he began to spin, until all the straw was gold. And when in the morning the king came and found all done according to his wish, he caused the wedding to be held at once, and the miller's pretty daughter became a queen.

In a year's time she brought a fine child into the world,

and thought no more of the little man; but one day he came suddenly into her room, and said,

"Now give me what you promised me."

The queen was terrified greatly, and offered the little man all the riches of the kingdom if he would only leave the child; but the little man said,

"No, I would rather have something living than all the treasures of the world."

Then the queen began to lament and to weep, so that the little man had pity upon her.

"I will give you three days," said he, "and if at the end of that time you cannot tell my name, you must give up the child to me."

Then the queen spent the whole night in thinking over all the names that she had ever heard, and sent a messenger through the land to ask far and wide for all the names that could be found. And when the little man came next day, (beginning with Caspar, Melchior, Balthazar) she repeated all she knew, and went through the whole list, but after each the little man said,

"That is not my name."

The second day the queen sent to inquire of all the neighbours what the servants were called, and told the little man all the most unusual and singular names, saying,

"Perhaps you are called Roast-ribs, or Sheepshanks, or Spindleshanks?" But he answered nothing but,

"That is not my name."

The third day the messenger came back again, and said,

"I have not been able to find one single new name; but as I passed through the woods I came to a high hill, and near it was a little house, and before the house burned a fire, and round the fire danced a comical little man, and he hopped on one leg and cried,

> "To-day do I bake, to-morrow I brew,
>   The day after that the queen's child comes in;
> And oh! I am glad that nobody knew
>   That the name I am called is Rumpelstiltskin!"

You cannot think how pleased the queen was to hear that name, and soon afterwards, when the little man walked in and said, "Now, Mrs. Queen, what is my name?" she said at first,

"Are you called Jack?"

"No," answered he.

"Are you called Harry?" she asked again.

"No," answered he. And then she said,

"Then perhaps your name is Rumpelstiltskin!"

"The devil told you that! the devil told you that!" cried the little man, and in his anger he stamped with his right foot so hard that it went into the ground above his knee; then he seized his left foot with both his hands in such a fury that he split in two, and there was an end of him.

Little Red Riding Hood

THERE WAS ONCE a sweet little maid, much beloved by everybody, but most of all by her grandmother, who never knew how to make enough of her. Once she sent her a little cloak of red velvet, and as it was very becoming to her, and she never wore anything else, people called her Little Red Riding Hood. One day her mother said to her,

"Come, Little Red Riding Hood, here are some cakes and a flask of wine for you to take to grandmother; she is weak and ill, and they will do her good. Make haste and start before it grows hot, and walk properly and nicely, and don't run, or you might fall and break the flask of wine, and there would be none left for grandmother. And when you go into her room, don't forget to say, Good morning, instead of staring about you."

"I will be sure to take care," said Little Red Riding Hood to her mother, and gave her hand upon it. Now the grandmother lived away in the wood, half-an-hour's walk from the village; and when Little Red Riding Hood had reached the wood, she met the wolf; but as she did not know what a bad sort of animal he was, she did not feel frightened.

"Good day, Little Red Riding Hood," said he.

"Thank you kindly, Wolf," answered she.

"Where are you going so early, Little Red Riding Hood?"

"To my grandmother's."

"What are you carrying under your apron?"

"Cakes and wine; we baked yesterday; and my grandmother is very weak and ill, so they will do her good, and strengthen her."

"Where does your grandmother live, Little Red Riding Hood?"

"A quarter of an hour's walk from here; her house stands beneath the three oak trees, and you may know it by the hazel bushes," said Little Red Riding Hood. The wolf thought to himself,

"That tender young thing would be a delicious morsel, and would taste better than the old one; I must manage somehow to get both of them."

Then he walked by Little Red Riding Hood a little while, and said,

"Little Red Riding Hood, just look at the pretty flowers that are growing all round you, and I don't think you are listening to the song of the birds; you are posting along just as if you were going to school, and it is so delightful out here in the wood."

Little Red Riding Hood glanced round her, and when she saw the sunbeams darting here and there through the trees, and lovely flowers everywhere, she thought to herself,

"If I were to take a fresh nosegay to my grandmother she would be very pleased, and it is so early in the day that I shall reach her in plenty of time"; and so she ran about in the wood, looking for flowers. And as she picked one she saw a still prettier one a little farther off, and so she went farther and farther into the wood. But the wolf went straight to the grandmother's house and knocked at the door.

"Who is there?" cried the grandmother.

"Little Red Riding Hood," he answered, "and I have brought you some cake and wine. Please open the door."

"Lift the latch," cried the grandmother; "I am too feeble to get up."

So the wolf lifted the latch, and the door flew open, and he fell on the grandmother and ate her up without saying one word. Then he drew on her clothes, put on her cap, lay down in her bed, and drew the curtains.

Little Red Riding Hood was all this time running about

among the flowers, and when she had gathered as many as she could hold, she remembered her grandmother, and set off to go to her. She was surprised to find the door standing open, and when she came inside she felt very strange, and thought to herself,

"Oh dear, how uncomfortable I feel, and I was so glad this morning to go to my grandmother!"

And when she said, "Good morning," there was no answer. Then she went up to the bed and drew back the curtains; there lay the grandmother with her cap pulled over her eyes, so that she looked very odd.

"O grandmother, what large ears you have got!"

"The better to hear with."

"O grandmother, what great eyes you have got!"

"The better to see with."

"O grandmother, what large hands you have got!"

"The better to take hold of you with."

"But, grandmother, what a terrible large mouth you have got!"

"The better to devour you!" And no sooner had the wolf said it than he made one bound from the bed, and swallowed up poor Little Red Riding Hood.

Then the wolf, having satisfied his hunger, lay down again in the bed, went to sleep, and began to snore loudly. The huntsman heard him as he was passing by the house, and thought,

"How the old woman snores—I had better see if there is anything the matter with her."

Then he went into the room, and walked up to the bed, and saw the wolf lying there.

"At last I find you, you old sinner!" said he; "I have been looking for you a long time." And he made up his mind that the wolf had swallowed the grandmother whole, and that she might yet be saved. So he did not fire, but took a pair of shears and began to split up the wolf's body. When he made a few snips Little Red Riding Hood appeared, and after a few more snips she jumped out and cried, "Oh, dear, how frightened I have been! it is so dark inside the wolf." And then out came the old grandmother, still living and breathing. But Little Red Riding Hood went and quickly fetched some large stones, with which she filled the wolf's body, so that when he waked up, and was going to rush away, the stones were so heavy that he sank down and fell dead.

They were all three very pleased. The huntsman took off the wolf's skin, and carried it home. The grandmother ate the cakes, and drank the wine, and held up her head again, and Little Red Riding Hood said to herself that she would never more stray about in the wood alone, but would mind what her mother told her.

It must also be related how a few days afterwards, when Little Red Riding Hood was again taking cakes to her grandmother, another wolf spoke to her, and wanted to tempt her to leave the path; but she was on her guard, and went straight on her way, and told her grandmother how that the wolf had met her, and wished her good-day, but had looked so wicked about the eyes that she thought if it had not been on the high road he would have devoured her.

"Come," said the grandmother, "we will shut the door, so that he may not get in."

Soon after came the wolf knocking at the door, and calling out, "Open the door, grandmother, I am Little Red Riding Hood, bringing you cakes." But they remained still, and did not open the door. After that the wolf slunk by the house, and got at last upon the roof to wait until Little Red Riding Hood should return home in the evening; then he meant to spring down upon her, and devour her in the darkness. But the grandmother discovered his plot. Now there stood before the house a great stone trough, and the grandmother said to the child, "Little Red Riding Hood, I was boiling sausages yesterday, so take the bucket, and carry away the water they were boiled in, and pour it into the trough."

And Little Red Riding Hood did so until the great trough

was quite full. When the smell of the sausages reached the nose of the wolf he snuffed it up, and looked round, and stretched out his neck so far that he lost his balance and began to slip, and he slipped down off the roof straight into the great trough, and was drowned. Then Little Red Riding Hood went cheerfully home, and came to no harm.

Tom Thumb

THERE WAS ONCE a poor countryman who used to sit in the chimney-corner all evening and poke the fire, while his wife sat at her spinning-wheel.

And he used to say,

"How dull it is without any children about us; our house is so quiet, and other people's houses so noisy and merry!"

"Yes," answered his wife, and sighed, "if we could only have one, and that one ever so little, no bigger than my thumb, how happy I should be! It would, indeed, be having our heart's desire."

Now, it happened that after a while the woman had a child who was perfect in all his limbs, but no bigger than a thumb. Then the parents said,

"He is just what we wished for, and we will love him very much," and they named him according to his stature, "Tom Thumb." And though they gave him plenty of nourishment, he grew no bigger, but remained exactly the same size as when he was first born; and he had very good faculties, and was very quick and prudent, so that all he did prospered.

One day his father made ready to go into the forest to cut wood, and he said, as if to himself,

"Now, I wish there was some one to bring the cart to meet me."

"O father," cried Tom Thumb, "I can bring the cart, let me alone for that, and in proper time, too!"

Then the father laughed, and said,

"How will you manage that? You are much too little to hold the reins."

"That has nothing to do with it, father; while my mother goes on with her spinning I will sit in the horse's ear and tell him where to go."

"Well," answered the father, "we will try it for once."

When it was time to set off, the mother went on spinning, after setting Tom Thumb in the horse's ear; and so he drove off, crying,

"Gee-up, gee-wo!"

So the horse went on quite as if his master were driving him, and drew the waggon along the right road to the wood.

Now it happened just as they turned a corner, and the little fellow was calling out "Gee-up!" that two strange men passed by.

"Look," said one of them, "how is this? There goes a waggon, and the driver is calling to the horse, and yet he is nowhere to be seen."

"It is very strange," said the other; "we will follow the waggon, and see where it belongs."

And the waggon went right through the wood, up to the place where the wood had been hewed. When Tom Thumb caught sight of his father, he cried out,

"Look father, here am I with the waggon; now, take me down."

The father held the horse with his left hand, and with the right he lifted down his little son out of the horse's ear, and Tom Thumb sat down on a stump, quite happy and content. When the two strangers saw him they were struck dumb with wonder. At last one of them, taking the other aside, said to him, "Look here, the little chap would make our fortune if we were to show him in the town for money. Suppose we buy him."

So they went up to the woodcutter, and said,

"Sell the little man to us; we will take care he shall come to no harm."

"No," answered the father; "he is the apple of my eye, and not for all the money in the world would I sell him."

But Tom Thumb, when he heard what was going on, climbed up by his father's coat tails, and, perching himself on his shoulder, he whispered in his ear,

"Father, you might as well let me go. I will soon come back again."

Then the father gave him up to the two men for a large piece of money. They asked him where he would like to sit.

"Oh, put me on the brim of your hat," said he. "There I can walk about and view the country, and be in no danger of falling off."

So they did as he wished, and when Tom Thumb had taken leave of his father, they set off all together. And they travelled on until it grew dusk, and the little fellow asked to be set down a little while for a change, and after some difficulty they consented. So the man took him down from his hat, and set him in a field by the roadside, and he ran away directly, and, after creeping about among the furrows, he slipped suddenly into a mouse-hole, just what he was looking for.

"Good evening, my masters, you can go home without me!" cried he to them, laughing. They ran up and felt about with their sticks in the mouse-hole, but in vain. Tom Thumb crept farther and farther in, and as it was growing dark, they had to make the best of their way home, full of vexation, and with empty purses.

When Tom Thumb found they were gone, he crept out of his hiding-place underground.

"It is dangerous work groping about these holes in the darkness," said he; "I might easily break my neck."

But by good fortune he came upon an empty snail shell.

"That's all right," said he. "Now I can get safely through the night"; and he settled himself down in it. Before he had time to get to sleep, he heard two men pass by, and one was saying to the other,

"How can we manage to get hold of the rich parson's gold and silver?"

"I can tell you how," cried Tom Thumb.

"How is this?" said one of the thieves, quite frightened, "I hear some one speak!"

So they stood still and listened, and Tom Thumb spoke again.

"Take me with you; I will show you how to do it!"

"Where are you, then?" asked they.

"Look about on the ground and notice where the voice comes from," answered he.

At last they found him, and lifted him up.

"You little elf," said they, "how can you help us?"

"Look here," answered he, "I can easily creep between the iron bars of the parson's room and hand out to you whatever you would like to have."

"Very well," said they, "we will try what you can do."

So when they came to the parsonage-house, Tom Thumb crept into the room, but cried out with all his might,

"Will you have all that is here?" So the thieves were terrified, and said,

"Do speak more softly, lest any one should be awaked."

But Tom Thumb made as if he did not hear them, and cried out again,

"What would you like? will you have all that is here?" so that the cook, who was sleeping in a room hard by, heard it, and raised herself in bed and listened. The thieves, however, in their fear of being discovered, had run back part of the way, but they took courage again, thinking that it was only a jest of the little fellow's. So they came back and whispered to him to be serious, and to hand them out something.

Then Tom Thumb called out once more as loud as he could,

"Oh yes, I will give it all to you, only put out your hands."

Then the listening maid heard him distinctly that time, and jumped out of bed, and burst open the door. The thieves ran off as if the wild huntsman were behind them;

but the maid, as she could see nothing, went to fetch a light. And when she came back with one, Tom Thumb had taken himself off, without being seen by her, into the barn; and the maid, when she had looked in every hole and corner and found nothing, went back to bed at last, and thought that she must have been dreaming with her eyes and ears open.

So Tom Thumb crept among the hay, and found a comfortable nook to sleep in, where he intended to remain until it was day, and then to go home to his father and mother. But other things were to befall him; indeed, there is nothing but trouble and worry in this world! The maid got up at dawn of day to feed the cows. The first place she went to was the barn, where she took up an armful of hay, and it happened to be the very heap in which Tom Thumb lay asleep. And he was so fast asleep, that he was aware of nothing, and never waked until he was in the mouth of the cow, who had taken him up with the hay.

"Oh dear," cried he, "how is it that I have got into a mill!" but he soon found out where he was, and he had to be very careful not to get between the cow's teeth, and at last he had to descend into the cow's stomach.

"The windows were forgotten when this little room was built," said he, "and the sunshine cannot get in; there is no light to be had."

His quarters were in every way unpleasant to him, and, what was the worst, new hay was constantly coming in, and the space was being filled up. At last he cried out in his extremity, as loud as he could,

"No more hay for me! no more hay for me!"

The maid was then milking the cow, and as she heard a voice, but could see no one, and as it was the same voice that she had heard in the night, she was so frightened that she fell off her stool, and spilt the milk. Then she ran in great haste to her master, crying,

"Oh, master dear, the cow spoke!"

"You must be crazy," answered her master, and he went himself to the cow-house to see what was the matter. No sooner had he put his foot inside the door, than Tom Thumb cried out again,

"No more hay for me! no more hay for me!"

Then the parson himself was frightened, supposing that a bad spirit had entered into the cow, and he ordered her to be put to death. So she was killed, but the stomach, where Tom Thumb was lying, was thrown upon a dunghill. Tom Thumb had great trouble to work his way out of it, and he had just made a space big enough for his head to go through, when a new misfortune happened. A hungry wolf ran up and swallowed the whole stomach at one gulp. But Tom Thumb did not lose courage. "Perhaps," thought he, "the wolf will listen to reason," and he cried out from the inside of the wolf,

"My dear wolf, I can tell you where to get a splendid meal!"

"Where is it to be had?" asked the wolf.

"In such and such a house, and you must creep into it through the drain, and there you will find cakes and bacon and broth, as much as you can eat," and he described to him his father's house. The wolf needed not to be told twice. He squeezed himself through the drain in the night, and feasted in the store-room to his heart's content. When, at last, he was satisfied, he wanted to go away again, but he had become so big, that to creep the same way back was impossible. This Tom Thumb had reckoned upon, and began to make a terrible din inside the wolf, crying and calling as loud as he could.

"Will you be quiet?" said the wolf; "you will wake the folks up!"

"Look here," cried the little man, "you are very well satisfied, and now I will do something for my own enjoyment," and began again to make all the noise he could. At last the father and mother were awakened, and they ran to the room-door and peeped through the chink, and when they saw a wolf in occupation, they ran and fetched weapons—the man an axe, and the wife a scythe.

"Stay behind," said the man, as they entered the room;

"when I have given him a blow, and it does not seem to have killed him, then you must cut at him with your scythe."

Then Tom Thumb heard his father's voice, and cried,

"Dear father, I am here in the wolf's inside."

Then the father called out full of joy,

"Thank heaven that we have found our dear child!" and told his wife to keep the scythe out of the way, lest Tom Thumb should be hurt with it. Then he drew near and struck the wolf such a blow on the head that he fell down dead; and then he fetched a knife and a pair of scissors, slit up the wolf's body, and let out the little fellow.

"Oh, what anxiety we have felt about you!" said the father.

"Yes, father, I have seen a good deal of the world, and I am very glad to breathe fresh air again."

"And where have you been all this time?" asked his father.

"Oh, I have been in a mouse-hole and a snail's shell, in a cow's stomach and a wolf's inside; now, I think, I will stay at home."

"And we will not part with you for all the kingdoms of the world," cried the parents, as they kissed and hugged their dear little Tom Thumb. And they gave him something to eat and drink, and a new suit of clothes, as his old ones were soiled with travel.

Rapunzel

THERE ONCE LIVED a man and his wife, who had long wished for a child, but in vain. Now there was at the back of their house a little window which overlooked a beautiful garden full of the finest vegetables and flowers; but there was a high wall all round it, and no one ventured into it, for it belonged to a witch of great might, and of whom all the world was afraid. One day that the wife was standing at the window, and looking into the garden, she saw a bed filled with the finest rampion; and it looked so fresh and green that she began to wish for some; and at length she longed for it greatly. This went on for days, and as she knew she could not get the rampion, she pined away, and grew pale and miserable. Then the man was uneasy, and asked,

"What is the matter, dear wife?"

"Oh," answered she, "I shall die unless I can have some of that rampion to eat that grows in the garden at the back of our house." The man, who loved her very much, thought to himself,

"Rather than lose my wife I will get some rampion, cost what it will."

So in the twilight he climbed over the wall into the witch's garden, plucked hastily a handful of rampion and brought it to his wife. She made a salad of it at once, and ate of it to her heart's content. But she liked it so much, and it tasted so good, that the next day she longed for it thrice as much as she had done before; if she was to have any rest the man must climb over the wall once more. So he went in the twilight again; and as he was climbing back, he saw, all at once, the witch standing before him, and was terribly frightened, as she cried, with angry eyes,

"How dare you climb over into my garden like a thief, and steal my rampion! it shall be the worse for you!"

"Oh," answered he, "be merciful rather than just, I have only done it through necessity; for my wife saw your rampion out of the window, and became possessed with so great a longing that she would have died if she could not have had some to eat." Then the witch said,

"If it is all as you say you may have as much rampion as you like, on one condition—the child that will come into the world must be given to me. It shall go well with the child, and I will care for it like a mother."

In his distress of mind the man promised everything; and when the time came when the child was born the witch appeared, and, giving the child the name of Rapunzel (which is the same as rampion), she took it away with her.

Rapunzel was the most beautiful child in the world. When she was twelve years old the witch shut her up in a tower in the midst of a wood, and it had neither steps nor door, only a small window above. When the witch wished to be let in, she would stand below and would cry,

"Rapunzel, Rapunzel! let down your hair!"

Rapunzel had beautiful long hair that shone like gold. When she heard the voice of the witch she would undo the fastening of the upper window, unbind the plaits of her hair, and let it down twenty ells below, and the witch would climb up by it.

After they had lived thus a few years it happened that as the King's son was riding through the wood, he came to the tower; and as he drew near he heard a voice singing so sweetly that he stood still and listened. It was Rapunzel in her loneliness trying to pass away the time with sweet songs. The King's son wished to go in to her, and sought to find a door in the tower, but there was none. So he rode home, but the song had entered into his heart, and every day he went into the wood and listened to it. Once, as he was standing there under a tree, he saw the witch come up, and listened while she called out,

"O Rapunzel, Rapunzel! let down your hair."

Then he saw how Rapunzel let down her long tresses, and how the witch climbed up by it and went in to her, and he said to himself,

"Since that is the ladder I will climb it, and seek my fortune." And the next day, as soon as it began to grow dusk, he went to the tower and cried,

"O Rapunzel, Rapunzel! let down your hair."

And she let down her hair, and the King's son climbed up by it.

Rapunzel was greatly terrified when she saw that a man had come in to her, for she had never seen one before; but the King's son began speaking so kindly to her, and told how her singing had entered into his heart, so that he could have no peace until he had seen her himself. Then Rapunzel forgot her terror, and when he asked her to take him for her husband, and she saw that he was young and beautiful, she thought to herself,

"I certainly like him very much better than old mother Gothel," and she put her hand into his hand, saying,

"I would willingly go with thee, but I do not know how I shall get out. When thou comest, bring each time a silken rope, and I will make a ladder, and when it is quite ready I will get down by it out of the tower, and thou shalt take me away on thy horse." They agreed that he should come to her every evening, as the old woman came in the daytime. So the witch knew nothing of all this until once Rapunzel said to her unwittingly,

"Mother Gothel, how is it that you climb up here so slowly, and the King's son is with me in a moment?"

"O wicked child," cried the witch, "what is this I hear! I thought I had hidden thee from all the world, and thou hast betrayed me!"

In her anger she seized Rapunzel by her beautiful hair,

struck her several times with her left hand, and then grasping a pair of shears in her right—snip, snap—the beautiful locks lay on the ground. And she was so hard-hearted that she took Rapunzel and put her in a waste and desert place, where she lived in great woe and misery.

The same day on which she took Rapunzel away she went back to the tower in the evening and made fast the severed locks of hair to the window-hasp, and the King's son came and cried,

"Rapunzel, Rapunzel! let down your hair."

Then she let the hair down, and the King's son climbed up, but instead of his dearest Rapunzel he found the witch looking at him with wicked glittering eyes.

"Aha!" cried she, mocking him, "you came for your darling, but the sweet bird sits no longer in the nest, and sings no more; the cat has got her, and will scratch out your eyes as well! Rapunzel is lost to you, you will see her no more."

The King's son was beside himself with grief, and in his agony he sprang from the tower; he escaped with life, but the thorns on which he fell put out his eyes. Then he wandered blind through the wood, eating nothing but roots and berries, and doing nothing but lament and weep for the loss of his dearest wife.

So he wandered several years in misery until at last he came to the desert place where Rapunzel lived with her twin-children that she had borne, a boy and a girl. At first he heard a voice that he thought he knew, and when he reached the place from which it seemed to come Rapunzel knew him, and fell on his neck and wept. And when her tears touched his eyes they became clear again, and he could see with them as well as ever.

Then he took her to his kingdom, where he was received with great joy, and there they lived long and happily.

Snow White

IT WAS THE middle of winter, and the snowflakes were falling like feathers from the sky, and a queen sat at her window working, and her embroidery frame was of ebony. And as she worked, gazing at times out on the snow, she pricked her finger, and there fell from it three drops of blood on the snow. And when she saw how bright and red it looked, she said to herself, "Oh that I had a child as white as snow, as red as blood, and as black as the wood of the embroidery frame!"

Not very long after she had a daughter, with a skin as white as snow, lips as red as blood, and hair as black as ebony, and she was named Snow White. And when she was born the queen died.

After a year had gone by the king took another wife, a beautiful woman, but proud and overbearing, and she could not bear to be surpassed in beauty by any one. She had a magic looking glass, and she used to stand before it, and look in it, and say,

> "Looking glass upon the wall,
> Who is fairest of us all?"

And the looking glass would answer,

> "You are fairest of them all."

And she was contented, for she knew that the looking glass spoke the truth.

Now, Snow White was growing prettier and prettier, and when she was seven years old she was as beautiful as day, far more so than the queen herself. So one day when the queen went to her mirror and said,

> "Looking glass upon the wall,
> Who is fairest of us all?"

It answered,

> "Queen, you are full fair, 'tis true,
> But Snow White fairer is than you."

This gave the queen a great shock, and she became yellow and green with envy, and from that hour her heart turned against Snow White, and she hated her. And envy and pride like ill weeds grew in her heart higher every day, until she had no peace day or night. At last she sent for a huntsman, and said,

"Take the child out into the woods, so that I may set eyes on her no more. You must put her to death, and bring me her heart for a token."

The huntsman consented, and led her away; but when he drew his cutlass to pierce Snow White's innocent heart, she began to weep, and to say,

"Oh, dear huntsman, do not take my life; I will go away into the wild wood, and never come home again."

And as she was so lovely the huntsman had pity on her, and said,

"Away with you then, poor child"; for he thought the wild animals would be sure to devour her, and it was as if a stone had been rolled away from his heart when he spared to put her to death. Just at that moment a young wild boar came running by, so he caught and killed it, and taking out its heart, he brought it to the queen for a token. And it was salted and cooked, and the wicked woman ate it up, thinking that there was an end of Snow White.

Now, when the poor child found herself quite alone in

the wild woods, she felt full of terror, even of the very leaves on the trees, and she did not know what to do for fright. Then she began to run over the sharp stones and through the thorn bushes, and the wild beasts after her, but they did her no harm. She ran as long as her feet would carry her; and when the evening drew near she came to a little house, and she went inside to rest. Everything there was very small, but as pretty and clean as possible. There stood the little table ready laid, and covered with a white cloth, and seven little plates, and seven knives and forks, and drinking cups. By the wall stood seven little beds, side by side, covered with clean white quilts. Snow White, being very hungry and thirsty, ate from each plate a little porridge and bread, and drank out of each little cup a drop of wine, so as not to finish up one portion alone. After that she felt so tired that she lay down on one of the beds, but it did not seem to suit her; one was too long, another too short, but at last the seventh was quite right; and so she lay down upon it, committed herself to heaven, and fell asleep.

When it was quite dark, the masters of the house came home. They were seven dwarfs, whose occupation was to dig underground among the mountains. When they had lighted their seven candles, and it was quite light in the little house, they saw that some one must have been in, as everything was not in the same order in which they left it. The first said,

"Who has been sitting in my little chair?"

The second said,

"Who has been eating from my little plate?"

The third said,

"Who has been taking my little loaf?"

The fourth said,

"Who has been tasting my porridge?"

The fifth said,

"Who has been using my little fork?"

The sixth said,

"Who has been cutting with my little knife?"

The seventh said,

"Who has been drinking from my little cup?"

Then the first one, looking round, saw a hollow in his bed, and cried,

"Who has been lying on my bed?"

And the others came running, and cried,

"Some one has been on our beds too!"

But when the seventh looked at his bed, he saw little Snow White lying there asleep. Then he told the others, who came running up, crying out in their astonishment, and holding up their seven little candles to throw a light upon Snow White.

"O goodness! O gracious!" cried they, "what beautiful child is this?" and were so full of joy to see her that they did not wake her, but let her sleep on. And the seventh dwarf slept with his comrades, an hour at a time with each, until the night had passed.

When it was morning, and Snow White awoke and saw the seven dwarfs, she was very frightened; but they seemed quite friendly, and asked her what her name was, and she told them; and then they asked how she came to be in their house. And she related to them how her stepmother had wished her to be put to death, and how the huntsman had spared her life, and how she had run the whole day long, until at last she had found their little house. Then the dwarfs said,

"If you will keep our house for us, and cook, and wash, and make the beds, and sew and knit, and keep everything tidy and clean, you may stay with us, and you shall lack nothing."

"With all my heart," said Snow White; and so she stayed, and kept the house in good order. In the morning the dwarfs went to the mountain to dig for gold; in the evening they came home, and their supper had to be ready for them. All the day long the maiden was left alone, and the good little dwarfs warned her, saying,

"Beware of your stepmother, she will soon know you are here. Let no one into the house."

Now the queen, having eaten Snow White's heart, as she supposed, felt quite sure that now she was the first and fairest, and so she came to her mirror, and said,

> "Looking glass upon the wall,
> Who is fairest of us all?"

And the glass answered,

> "Queen, thou art of beauty rare,
> But Snow White living in the glen
> With the seven little men
> Is a thousand times more fair."

Then she was very angry, for the glass always spoke the truth, and she knew that the huntsman must have deceived her, and that Snow White must still be living. And she thought and thought how she could manage to make an end of her, for as long as she was not the fairest in the land, envy left her no rest. At last she thought of a plan; she painted her face and dressed herself like an old pedlar woman, so that no one would have known her. In this disguise she went across the seven mountains, until she came to the house of the seven little dwarfs, and she knocked at the door and cried,

"Fine wares to sell! fine wares to sell!"

Snow White peeped out of the window and cried,

"Good-day, good woman, what have you to sell?"

"Good wares, fine wares," answered she, "laces of all colours"; and she held up a piece that was woven of variegated silk.

"I need not be afraid of letting in this good woman," thought Snow White, and she unbarred the door and bought the pretty lace.

"What a figure you are, child!" said the old woman, "come and let me lace you properly for once."

Snow White, suspecting nothing, stood up before her, and let her lace her with the new lace; but the old woman laced so quick and tight that it took Snow White's breath away, and she fell down as dead.

"Now you have done with being the fairest," said the old woman as she hastened away.

Not long after that, towards evening, the seven dwarfs came home, and were terrified to see their dear Snow White lying on the ground, without life or motion; they raised her up, and when they saw how tightly she was laced they cut the lace in two; then she began to draw breath, and little by little she returned to life. When the dwarfs heard what had happened they said,

"The old pedlar woman was no other than the wicked queen; you must beware of letting any one in when we are not here!"

And when the wicked woman got home she went to her glass and said,

> "Looking glass against the wall,
>   Who is fairest of us all?"

And it answered as before,

> "Queen, thou art of beauty rare,
>   But Snow White living in the glen
>   With the seven little men
>   Is a thousand times more fair."

When she heard that she was so struck with surprise that all the blood left her heart, for she knew that Snow White must still be living.

"But now," said she, "I will think of something that will be her ruin." And by witchcraft she made a poisoned comb. Then she dressed herself up to look like another different sort of old woman. So she went across the seven mountains and came to the house of the seven dwarfs, and knocked at the door and cried,

"Good wares to sell! good wares to sell!"

Snow White looked out and said,

"Go away, I must not let anybody in."

"But you are not forbidden to look," said the old woman, taking out the poisoned comb and holding it up. It pleased the poor child so much that she was tempted to open the door; and when the bargain was made the old woman said,

"Now, for once your hair shall be properly combed."

Poor Snow White, thinking no harm, let the old woman do as she would, but no sooner was the comb put in her hair than the poison began to work, and the poor girl fell down senseless.

"Now, you paragon of beauty," said the wicked woman, "this is the end of you," and went off. By good luck it was now near evening, and the seven little dwarfs came home. When they saw Snow White lying on the ground as dead, they thought directly that it was the stepmother's doing, and looked about, found the poisoned comb, and no sooner had they drawn it out of her hair than Snow White came to herself, and related all that had passed. Then they warned her once more to be on her guard, and never again to let any one in at the door.

And the queen went home and stood before the looking glass and said,

> "Looking glass against the wall,
> Who is fairest of us all?"

And the looking glass answered as before,

> "Queen, thou art of beauty rare,
> But Snow White living in the glen
> With the seven little men
> Is a thousand times more fair."

When she heard the looking glass speak thus she trembled and shook with anger.

"Snow White shall die," cried she, "though it should cost me my own life!" And then she went to a secret lonely chamber, where no one was likely to come, and there she made a poisonous apple. It was beautiful to look upon, being white with red cheeks, so that any one who should see it must long for it, but whoever ate even a little bit of it must die. When the apple was ready she painted her face and clothed herself like a peasant woman, and went across the seven mountains to where the seven dwarfs lived. And when she knocked at the door Snow White put her head out of the window and said,

"I dare not let anybody in; the seven dwarfs told me not."

"All right," answered the woman; "I can easily get rid of my apples elsewhere. There, I will give you one."

"No," answered Snow White, "I dare not take anything."

"Are you afraid of poison?" said the woman, "look here, I will cut the apple in two pieces; you shall have the red side, I will have the white one."

For the apple was so cunningly made, that all the poison was in the rosy half of it. Snow White longed for the beautiful apple, and as she saw the peasant woman eating a piece of it she could no longer refrain, but stretched out her hand and took the poisoned half. But no sooner had she taken a morsel of it into her mouth that she fell to the earth as dead. And the queen, casting on her a terrible glance, laughed aloud and cried,

"As white as snow, as red as blood, as black as ebony! this time the dwarfs will not be able to bring you to life again."

And when she went home and asked the looking glass,

> "Looking glass against the wall,
> Who is fairest of us all?"

at last it answered,

"You are the fairest now of all."

Then her envious heart had peace, as much as an envious heart can have.

The dwarfs, when they came home in the evening,

found Snow White lying on the ground, and there came no breath out of her mouth, and she was dead. They lifted her up, sought if anything poisonous was to be found, cut her laces, combed her hair, washed her with water and wine, but all was of no avail, the poor child was dead, and remained dead. Then they laid her on a bier, and sat all seven of them round it, and wept and lamented three whole days. And then they would have buried her, but that she looked still as if she were living, with her beautiful blooming cheeks. So they said,

"We cannot hide her away in the black ground." And they had made a coffin of clear glass, so as to be looked into from all sides, and they laid her in it, and wrote in golden letters upon it her name, and that she was a king's daughter. Then they set the coffin out upon the mountain, and one of them always remained by it to watch. And the birds came too, and mourned for Snow White, first an owl, then a raven, and lastly, a dove.

Now, for a long while Snow White lay in the coffin and never changed, but looked as if she were asleep, for she was still as white as snow, as red as blood, and her hair was as black as ebony. It happened, however, that one day a king's son rode through the wood and up to the dwarfs' house, which was near it. He saw on the mountain the coffin, and beautiful Snow White within it, and he read what was written in golden letters upon it. Then he said to the dwarfs,

"Let me have the coffin, and I will give you whatever you like to ask for it."

But the dwarfs told him that they could not part with it for all the gold in the world. But he said,

"I beseech you to give it me, for I cannot live without looking upon Snow White; if you consent I will bring you to great honour, and care for you as if you were my brethren."

When he so spoke the good little dwarfs had pity upon him and gave him the coffin, and the king's son called his servants and bid them carry it away on their shoulders.

Now it happened that as they were going along they stumbled over a bush, and with the shaking the bit of poisoned apple flew out of her throat. It was not long before she opened her eyes, threw up the cover of the coffin, and sat up, alive and well.

"Oh dear! where am I?" cried she. The king's son answered, full of joy, "You are near me," and, relating all that had happened, he said,

"I would rather have you than anything in the world; come with me to my father's castle and you shall be my bride."

And Snow White was kind, and went with him, and their wedding was held with pomp and great splendour.

But Snow White's wicked stepmother was also bidden to the feast, and when she had dressed herself in beautiful clothes she went to her looking glass and said,

> "Looking glass upon the wall,
> Who is fairest of us all?"

The looking glass answered,

> "O Queen, although you are of beauty rare,
> The young bride is a thousand times more fair."

Then she railed and cursed, and was beside herself with disappointment and anger. First she thought she would not go to the wedding; but then she felt she should have no peace until she went and saw the bride. And when she saw her she knew her for Snow White, and could not stir from the place for anger and terror. For they had ready red-hot iron shoes, in which she had to dance until she fell down dead.

The Queen Bee

TWO KING'S SONS once started to seek adventures, and fell into a wild, reckless way of living, and gave up all thoughts of going home again. Their third and youngest brother, who was called Witling, and had remained behind, started off to seek them; and when at last he found them, they jeered at his simplicity in thinking that he could make his way in the world, while they who were so much cleverer were unsuccessful. But they all three went on together until they came to an ant hill, which the two eldest brothers wished to stir up, that they might see the little ants hurry about in their fright and carrying off their eggs, but Witling said,

"Leave the little creatures alone, I will not suffer them to be disturbed."

And they went on farther until they came to a lake, where a number of ducks were swimming about. The two eldest brothers wanted to catch a couple and cook them, but Witling would not allow it, and said, "Leave the creatures alone, I will not suffer them to be killed."

And then they came to a bee's nest in a tree, and there was so much honey in it that it overflowed and ran down the trunk. The two eldest brothers then wanted to make a fire beneath the tree, that the bees might be stifled by the smoke, and then they could get at the honey. But Witling prevented them, saying,

"Leave the little creatures alone, I will not suffer them to be stifled."

At last the three brothers came to a castle where there were in the stables many horses standing, all of stone, and the brothers went through all the rooms until they came to a door at the end secured with three locks, and in the middle of the door a small opening through which they could look into the room. And they saw a little grey-haired man sitting at a table. They called out to him once, twice, and he did not hear, but at the third time he got up, undid the locks, and came out. Without speaking a word he led them to a table loaded with all sorts of good things, and when they had eaten and drunk he showed to each his bedchamber. The next morning the little grey man came to the eldest brother, and beckoning him, brought him to a table of stone, on which were written three things directing by what means the castle could be delivered from its enchantment. The first thing was, that in the wood under the moss lay the pearls belonging to the princess—a thousand in number—and they were to be sought for and collected, and if he who should undertake the task had not finished it by sunset,—if but one pearl were missing,—he must be turned to stone. So the eldest brother went out, and searched all day, but at the end of it he had only found one hundred; just as was said on the table of stone came to pass and he was turned into stone. The second brother undertook the adventure next day, but it fared with him no better than with the first; he found two hundred pearls, and was turned into stone.

And so at last it was Witling's turn, and he began to search in the moss; but it was a very tedious business to find the pearls, and he grew so out of heart that he sat down on a stone and began to weep. As he was sitting thus, up came the ant king with five thousand ants, whose lives had been saved through Witling's pity, and it was not very long before the little insects had collected all the pearls and put them in a heap.

Now the second thing ordered by the table of stone was to get the key of the princess's sleeping chamber out of the lake.

And when Witling came to the lake, the ducks whose lives he had saved came swimming, and dived below, and brought up the key from the bottom. The third thing that had to be done was the most difficult, and that was to choose out the youngest and loveliest of the three princesses, as they lay sleeping. All bore a perfect resemblance each to the other, and only differed in this, that before they went to sleep each one had eaten a different sweetmeat,—the eldest a piece of sugar, the second a little syrup, and the third a spoonful of honey. Now the Queen bee of those bees that Witling had protected from the fire came at this moment, and trying the lips of all three, settled on those of the one that had eaten honey, and so it was that the king's son knew which to choose. Then the spell was broken; every one awoke from stony sleep, and took their right form again.

And Witling married the youngest and loveliest princess, and became king after her father's death. But his two brothers had to put up with the two other sisters.

The Fisherman and His Wife

THERE WAS ONCE a fisherman and his wife who lived together in a hovel by the seashore, and the fisherman went out every day with his hook and line to catch fish, and he angled and angled.

One day he was sitting with his rod and looking into the clear water, and he sat and sat.

At last down went the line to the bottom of the water, and when he drew it up he found a great flounder on the hook. And the flounder said to him,

"Fisherman, listen to me; let me go, I am not a real fish but an enchanted prince. What good shall I be to you if you land me? I shall not taste well; so put me back into the water again, and let me swim away."

"Well," said the fisherman, "no need of so many words about the matter, as you can speak I had much rather let you swim away."

Then he put him back into the clear water, and the flounder sank to the bottom, leaving a long streak of blood behind him. Then the fisherman got up and went home to his wife in their hovel.

"Well, husband," said the wife, "have you caught nothing today?"

"No," said the man—"that is, I did catch a flounder, but as he said he was an enchanted prince, I let him go again."

"Then, did you wish for nothing?" said the wife.

"No," said the man; "what should I wish for?"

"Oh dear!" said the wife; "and it is so dreadful always to

70

live in this evil-smelling hovel; you might as well have wished for a little cottage; go again and call him; tell him we want a little cottage, I daresay he will give it us; go, and be quick."

And when he went back, the sea was green and yellow, and not nearly so clear. So he stood and said,

> "O man, O man!—if man you be,
>   Or flounder, flounder, in the sea—
>   Such a tiresome wife I've got,
>   For she wants what I do not."

Then the flounder came swimming up, and said,

"Now then, what does she want?"

"Oh," said the man, "you know when I caught you my wife says I ought to have wished for something. She does not want to live any longer in the hovel, and would rather have a cottage."

"Go home with you," said the flounder, "she has it already."

So the man went home, and found, instead of the hovel, a little cottage, and his wife was sitting on a bench before the door. And she took him by the hand, and said to him,

"Come in and see if this is not a great improvement."

So they went in, and there was a little houseplace and a beautiful little bedroom, a kitchen and larder, with all sorts of furniture, and iron and brass ware of the very best. And at the back was a little yard with fowls and ducks, and a little garden full of green vegetables and fruit.

"Look," said the wife, "is not that nice?"

"Yes," said the man, "if this can only last we shall be very well contented."

"We will see about that," said the wife. And after a meal they went to bed.

So all went well for a week or fortnight, when the wife said,

"Look here, husband, the cottage is really too confined,

and the yard and garden are so small; I think the flounder had better get us a larger house; I should like very much to live in a large stone castle; so go to your fish and he will send us a castle."

"O my dear wife," said the man, "the cottage is good enough; what do we want a castle for?"

"We want one," said the wife; "go along with you; the flounder can give us one."

"Now, wife," said the man, "the flounder gave us the cottage; I do not like to go to him again, he may be angry."

"Go along," said the wife, "he might just as well give us it as not; do as I say!"

The man felt very reluctant and unwilling; and he said to himself,

"It is not the right thing to do"; nevertheless he went.

So when he came to the seaside, the water was purple and dark blue and grey and thick, and not green and yellow as before. And he stood and said,

> "O man, O man!—if man you be,
>   Or flounder, flounder, in the sea—
>   Such a tiresome wife I've got,
>   For she wants what I do not."

"Now then, what does she want?" said the flounder.

"Oh," said the man, half frightened, "she wants to live in a large stone castle."

"Go home with you, she is already standing before the door," said the flounder.

Then the man went home, as he supposed, but when he got there, there stood in the place of the cottage a great castle of stone, and his wife was standing on the steps, about to go in; so she took him by the hand, and said,

"Let us enter."

With that he went in with her, and in the castle was a great hall with a marble pavement, and there were a great many servants, who led them through large doors, and the passages were decked with tapestry, and the rooms with golden chairs and tables, and crystal chandeliers hanging from the ceiling; and all the rooms had carpets. And the tables were covered with eatables and the best wine for any one who wanted them. And at the back of the house was a great stableyard for horses and cattle, and carriages of the finest; besides, there was a splendid large garden, with the most beautiful flowers and fine fruit trees, and a pleasance full half a mile long, with deer and oxen and sheep, and everything that heart could wish for.

"There!" said the wife, "is not this beautiful?"

"Oh yes," said the man, "if it will only last we can live in this fine castle and be very well contented."

"We will see about that," said the wife, "in the meanwhile we will sleep upon it." With that they went to bed.

The next morning the wife was awake first, just at the break of day, and she looked out and saw from her bed the beautiful country lying all round. The man took no notice of it, so she poked him in the side with her elbow, and said,

"Husband, get up and just look out of the window. Look, just think if we could be king over all this country. Just go to your fish and tell him we should like to be king."

"Now, wife," said the man, "what should we be kings for? I don't want to be king."

"Well," said the wife, "if you don't want to be king, I will be king."

"Now, wife," said the man, "what do you want to be king for? I could not ask him such a thing."

"Why not?" said the wife, "you must go directly all the same; I must be king."

So the man went, very much put out that his wife should want to be king.

"It is not the right thing to do—not at all the right thing," thought the man. He did not at all want to go, and yet he went all the same.

And when he came to the sea the water was quite dark grey, and rushed far inland, and had an ill smell. And he stood and said,

"O man, O man!—if man you be,
  Or flounder, flounder, in the sea—
  Such a tiresome wife I've got,
  For she wants what I do not."

"Now then, what does she want?" said the fish.

"Oh dear!" said the man, "she wants to be king."

"Go home with you, she is so already," said the fish.

So the man went back, and as he came to the palace he saw it was very much larger, and had great towers and splendid gateways; the herald stood before the door, and a number of soldiers with kettle-drums and trumpets.

And when he came inside everything was of marble and gold, and there were many curtains with great golden tassels. Then he went through the doors of the saloon to where the great throne-room was, and there was his wife sitting upon a throne of gold and diamonds, and she had a great golden crown on, and the sceptre in her hand was of pure gold and jewels, and on each side stood six pages in a row, each one a head shorter than the other. So the man went up to her and said,

"Well, wife, so now you are king!"

"Yes," said the wife, "now I am king."

So then he stood and looked at her, and when he had gazed at her for some time he said,

"Well, wife, this is fine for you to be king! now there is nothing more to wish for."

"O husband!" said the wife, seeming quite restless, "I am tired of this already. Go to your fish and tell him that now I am king I must be emperor."

"Now, wife," said the man, "what do you want to be emperor for?"

"Husband," said she, "go and tell the fish I want to be emperor."

"Oh dear!" said the man, "he could not do it—I cannot ask him such a thing. There is but one emperor at a time; the fish can't possibly make any one emperor—indeed he can't."

"Now, look here," said the wife, "I am king, and you are only my husband, so will you go at once? Go along! for if he was able to make me king he is able to make me emperor; and I will and must be emperor, so go along!"

So he was obliged to go; and as he went he felt very uncomfortable about it, and he thought to himself,

"It is not at all the right thing to do; to want to be emperor is really going too far; the flounder will soon be beginning to get tired of this."

With that he came to the sea, and the water was quite black and thick, and the foam flew, and the wind blew, and the man was terrified. But he stood and said,

> "O man, O man!—if man you be,
>   Or flounder, flounder, in the sea—
>   Such a tiresome wife I've got,
>   For she wants what I do not."

"What is it now?" said the fish.

"Oh dear!" said the man, "my wife wants to be emperor."

"Go home with you," said the fish, "she is emperor already."

So the man went home, and found the castle adorned with polished marble and alabaster figures, and golden gates. The troops were being marshalled before the door, and they were blowing trumpets and beating drums and cymbals; and when he entered he saw barons and earls and dukes waiting about like servants; and the doors were of bright gold. And he saw his wife sitting upon a throne made of one entire piece of gold, and it was about two miles high; and she had a great golden crown on, which was about three yards high, set with brilliants and car-buncles; and in one hand she held the sceptre, and in the other the globe; and on both sides of her stood pages in two rows, all arranged according to their size, from the most enormous giant of two miles high to the tiniest dwarf of the size of my little finger; and before her stood earls and dukes in crowds. So the man went up to her and said,

"Well, wife, so now you are emperor."

"Yes," said she, "now I am emperor."

Then he went and sat down and had a good look at her, and then he said,

"Well now, wife, there is nothing left to be, now you are emperor."

"What are you talking about, husband?" said she; "I am emperor, and next I will be pope! so go and tell the fish so."

"Oh dear!" said the man, "what is it that you don't want? You can never become pope; there is but one pope in Christendom, and the fish can't possibly do it."

"Husband," said she, "no more words about it; I must and will be pope; so go along to the fish."

"Now, wife," said the man, "how can I ask him such a thing? it is too bad—it is asking a little too much; and, besides, he could not do it."

"What rubbish!" said the wife; "if he could make me an emperor he can make me pope. Go along and ask him; I am emperor, and you are only my husband, so go you must."

So he went, feeling very frightened, and he shivered and shook, and his knees trembled; and there arose a great wind, and the clouds flew by, and it grew very dark, and the sea rose mountains high, and the ships were tossed about, and the sky was partly blue in the middle, but at the sides very dark and red, as in a great tempest. And he felt very despondent, and stood trembling and said,

> "O man, O man!—if man you be,
>   Or flounder, flounder, in the sea—
>   Such a tiresome wife I've got,
>   For she wants what I do not."

"Well, what now?" said the fish.

"Oh dear!" said the man, "she wants to be pope."

"Go home with you, she is pope already," said the fish.

So he went home, and he found himself before a great church, with palaces all round. He had to make his way through a crowd of people; and when he got inside he found the place lighted up with thousands and thousands of lights; and his wife was clothed in a golden garment, and sat upon a very high throne, and had three golden crowns on, all in the greatest priestly pomp; and on both sides of her there stood two rows of lights of all sizes— from the size of the longest tower to the smallest rush-light, and all the emperors and kings were kneeling before her and kissing her foot.

"Well, wife," said the man, and sat and stared at her, "so you are pope."

"Yes," said she, "now I am pope!"

And he went on gazing at her till he felt dazzled, as if he were sitting in the sun. And after a little time he said,

"Well, now, wife, what is there left to be, now you are pope?"

And she sat up very stiff and straight, and said nothing.

And he said again, "Well, wife, I hope you are contented at last with being pope; you can be nothing more."

"We will see about that," said the wife. With that they both went to bed; but she was as far as ever from being contented, and she could not get to sleep for thinking of what she should like to be next.

The husband, however, slept as fast as a top after his busy day; but the wife tossed and turned from side to side the whole night through, thinking all the while what she could be next, but nothing would occur to her; and when she saw the red dawn she slipped off the bed, and sat before the window to see the sun rise, and as it came up she said,

"Ah, I have it! what if I should make the sun and moon to rise—husband!" she cried, and stuck her elbow in his ribs, "wake up, and go to your fish, and tell him I want power over the sun and moon."

The man was so fast asleep that when he started up he fell out of bed. Then he shook himself together, and opened his eyes and said,

"Oh,—wife, what did you say?"

"Husband," said she, "if I cannot get the power of making the sun and moon rise when I want them, I shall never have another quiet hour. Go to the fish and tell him so."

"O wife!" said the man, and fell on his knees to her, "the fish can really not do that for you. I grant you he could make you emperor and pope; do be contented with that, I beg of you."

And she became wild with impatience, and screamed out,

"I can wait no longer, go at once!"

And so off he went as well as he could for fright. And a dreadful storm arose, so that he could hardly keep his feet; and the houses and trees were blown down, and the mountains trembled, and rocks fell in the sea; the sky was quite black, and it thundered and lightened; and the waves, crowned with foam, ran mountains high. So he cried out, without being able to hear his own words,

> "O man, O man!—if man you be,
> Or flounder, flounder, in the sea—
> Such a tiresome wife I've got,
> For she wants what I do not."

"Well, what now?" said the flounder.

"Oh dear!" said the man, "she wants to order about the sun and moon."

"Go home with you!" said the flounder, "you will find her in the old hovel."

And there they are sitting to this very day.

The Brave Little Tailor

ONE SUMMER MORNING a little tailor was sitting on his board near the window, and working cheerfully with all his might, when an old woman came down the street crying,

"Good jelly to sell! good jelly to sell!"

The cry sounded pleasant in the little tailor's ears, so he put his head out of the window, and called out,

"Here, my good woman—come here, if you want a customer."

So the poor woman climbed the steps with her heavy basket, and was obliged to unpack and display all her pots to the tailor. He looked at every one of them, and lifting all the lids, applied his nose to each, and said at last,

"The jelly seems pretty good; you may weigh me out four half ounces, or I don't mind having a quarter of a pound."

The woman, who had expected to find a good customer, gave him what he asked for, but went off angry and grumbling.

"This jelly is the very thing for me," cried the little tailor; "it will give me strength and cunning"; and he took down the bread from the cupboard, cut a whole round of the loaf, and spread the jelly on it, laid it near him, and went on stitching more gallantly than ever. All the while the scent of the sweet jelly was spreading throughout the room, where there were quantities of flies, who were attracted by it and flew to partake.

"Now then, who asked you to come?" said the tailor, and drove the unbidden guests away. But the flies, not understanding his language, were not to be got rid of like that, and returned in larger numbers than before. Then the tailor, not being able to stand it any longer, took from his chimney corner a ragged cloth, and saying,

"Now, I'll let you have it!" beat it among them unmercifully. When he ceased, and counted the slain, he found seven lying dead before him.

"This is indeed somewhat," he said, wondering at his own gallantry; "the whole town shall know this."

So he hastened to cut out a belt, and he stitched it, and put on it in large capitals "Seven at one blow!"

"—The town did I say!" said the little tailor; "the whole world shall know it!" And his heart quivered with joy, like a lamb's tail.

The tailor fastened the belt round him, and began to think of going out into the world, for his workshop seemed too small for his worship. So he looked about in all the house for something that it would be useful to take with him, but he found nothing but an old cheese, which he put in his pocket. Outside the door he noticed that a bird had got caught in the bushes, so he took that and put it in his pocket with the cheese. Then he set out gallantly on his way, and as he was light and active he felt no fatigue. The way led over a mountain, and when he reached the topmost peak he saw a terrible giant sitting there, and looking about him at his ease. The tailor went bravely up to him, called out to him, and said,

"Comrade, good day! there you sit looking over the wide world! I am on the way thither to seek my fortune: have you a fancy to go with me?"

The giant looked at the tailor contemptuously, and said,

"You little rascal! you miserable fellow!"

"That may be!" answered the little tailor, and undoing his coat he showed the giant his belt; "you can read there whether I am a man or not!"

The giant read: "Seven at one blow!" and thinking it

meant men that the tailor had killed, felt at once more respect for the little fellow. But as he wanted to prove him, he took up a stone and squeezed it so hard that water came out of it.

"Now you can do that," said the giant,—"that is, if you have the strength for it."

"That's not much," said the little tailor, "I call that play," and he put his hand in his pocket and took out the cheese and squeezed it, so that the whey ran out of it.

"Well," said he, "what do you think of that?"

The giant did not know what to say to it, for he could not have believed it of the little man. Then the giant took up a stone and threw it so high that it was nearly out of sight.

"Now, little fellow, suppose you do that!"

"Well thrown," said the tailor; "but the stone fell back to earth again,—I will throw you one that will never come back." So he felt in his pocket, took out the bird, and threw it into the air. And the bird, when it found itself at liberty, took wing, flew off, and returned no more.

"What do you think of that, comrade?" asked the tailor.

"There is no doubt that you can throw," said the giant; "but we will see if you can carry."

He led the little tailor to a mighty oak tree which had been felled, and was lying on the ground, and said,

"Now, if you are strong enough, help me to carry this tree out of the wood."

"Willingly," answered the little man; "you take the trunk on your shoulders, I will take the branches with all their foliage, that is much the most difficult."

So the giant took the trunk on his shoulders, and the tailor seated himself on a branch, and the giant, who could not see what he was doing, had the whole tree to carry, and the little man on it as well. And the little man was very cheerful and merry, and whistled the tune: *"There were three tailors riding by,"* as if carrying the tree was mere child's play. The giant, when he had struggled on under his heavy load a part of the way, was tired out, and cried,

"Look here, I must let go the tree!"

The tailor jumped off quickly, and taking hold of the tree with both arms, as if he were carrying it, said to the giant,

"You see you can't carry the tree though you are such a big fellow!"

They went on together a little farther, and presently they came to a cherry tree, and the giant took hold of the topmost branches, where the ripest fruit hung, and pulling them downwards, gave them to the tailor to hold, bidding him eat. But the little tailor was much too weak to hold the tree, and as the giant let go, the tree sprang back, and the tailor was caught up into the air. And when he dropped down again without any damage, the giant said to him,

"How is this? haven't you strength enough to hold such a weak sprig as that?"

"It is not strength that is lacking," answered the little tailor; "how should it to one who has slain seven at one blow! I just jumped over the tree because the hunters are shooting down there in the bushes. You jump it too, if you can."

The giant made the attempt, and not being able to vault the tree, he remained hanging in the branches, so that once more the little tailor got the better of him. Then said the giant,

"As you are such a gallant fellow, suppose you come with me to our den, and stay the night."

The tailor was quite willing, and he followed him. When they reached the den there sat some other giants by the fire, and each had a roasted sheep in his hand, and was eating it. The little tailor looked round and thought,

"There is more elbow-room here than in my workshop."

And the giant showed him a bed, and told him he had better lie down upon it and go to sleep. The bed was, however, too big for the tailor, so he did not stay in it, but crept into a corner to sleep. As soon as it was midnight the giant got up, took a great staff of iron and beat the bed through with one stroke, and supposed he had made an

end of that grasshopper of a tailor. Very early in the morning the giants went into the wood and forgot all about the
little tailor, and when they saw him coming after them
alive and merry, they were terribly frightened, and, thinking he was going to kill them, they ran away in all haste.

So the little tailor marched on, always following his
nose. And after he had gone a great way he entered the
courtyard belonging to a King's palace, and there he felt
so overpowered with fatigue that he lay down and fell
asleep. In the meanwhile came various people, who
looked at him very curiously, and read on his belt, "Seven
at one blow!"

"Oh!" said they, "why should this great lord come here
in time of peace? what a mighty champion he must be."

Then they went and told the King about him, and they
thought that if war should break out what a worthy and
useful man he would be, and that he ought not to be
allowed to depart at any price. The King then summoned
his council, and sent one of his courtiers to the little tailor to beg him, so soon as he should wake up, to consent
to serve in the King's army. So the messenger stood and
waited at the sleeper's side until his limbs began to
stretch, and his eyes to open, and then he carried his
answer back. And the answer was,

"That was the reason for which I came," said the little
tailor, "I am ready to enter the King's service."

So he was received into it very honourably, and a sepa-
rate dwelling set apart for him.

But the rest of the soldiers were very much set against
the little tailor, and they wished him a thousand miles
away.

"What shall be done about it?" they said among themselves; "if we pick a quarrel and fight with him then seven
of us will fall at each blow. That will be of no good to us."

So they came to a resolution, and went all together to
the King to ask for their discharge.

"We never intended," said they, "to serve with a man
who kills seven at a blow."

The King felt sorry to lose all his faithful servants because of one man, and he wished that he had never seen him, and would willingly get rid of him if he might. But he did not dare to dismiss the little tailor for fear he should kill all the King's people, and place himself upon the throne. He thought a long while about it, and at last made up his mind what to do. He sent for the little tailor, and told him that as he was so great a warrior he had a proposal to make to him. He told him that in a wood in his dominions dwelt two giants, who did great damage by robbery, murder, and fire, and that no man durst go near them for fear of his life. But that if the tailor should over-come and slay both these giants the King would give him his only daughter in marriage, and half his kingdom as dowry, and that a hundred horsemen should go with him to give him assistance.

"That would be something for a man like me!" thought the little tailor, "a beautiful princess and half a kingdom are not to be had every day," and he said to the King,

"Oh yes, I can soon overcome the giants, and yet have no need of the hundred horsemen; he who can kill seven at one blow has no need to be afraid of two."

So the little tailor set out, and the hundred horsemen followed him. When he came to the border of the wood he said to his escort,

"Stay here while I go to attack the giants."

Then he sprang into the wood, and looked about him right and left. After a while he caught sight of the two giants; they were lying down under a tree asleep, and snoring so that all the branches shook. The little tailor, all alive, filled both his pockets with stones and climbed up into the tree, and made his way to an overhanging bough, so that he could seat himself just above the sleepers; and from there he let one stone after another fall on the chest of one of the giants. For a long time the giant was quite unaware of this, but at last he waked up and pushed his comrade, and said,

"What are you hitting me for?"

"You are dreaming," said the other, "I am not touching

you." And they composed themselves again to sleep, and the tailor let fall a stone on the other giant.

"What can that be?" cried he, "what are you casting at me?"

"I am casting nothing at you," answered the first, grumbling.

They disputed about it for a while, but as they were tired, they gave it up at last, and their eyes closed once more. Then the little tailor began his game anew, picked out a heavier stone and threw it down with force upon the first giant's chest.

"This is too much!" cried he, and sprang up like a madman and struck his companion such a blow that the tree shook above them. The other paid him back with ready coin, and they fought with such fury that they tore up trees by their roots to use for weapons against each other, so that at last they both of them lay dead upon the ground. And now the little tailor got down.

"Another piece of luck!" said he—"that the tree I was sitting in did not get torn up too, or else I should have had to jump like a squirrel from one tree to another."

Then he went back to the horsemen and said,

"The deed is done, I have made an end of both of them: but it went hard with me, in the struggle they rooted up trees to defend themselves, but it was of no use, they had to do with a man who can kill seven at one blow."

"Then are you not wounded?" asked the horsemen.

"Nothing of the sort!" answered the tailor, "I have not turned a hair."

The horsemen still would not believe it, and rode into the wood to see, and there they found the giants and all about them lying the uprooted trees.

The little tailor then claimed the promised boon, but the King repented him of his offer, and he sought again how to rid himself of the hero.

"Before you can possess my daughter and the half of my kingdom," said he to the tailor, "you must perform another heroic act. In the wood lives a unicorn who does great damage; you must secure him."

"A unicorn does not strike more terror into me than two giants. Seven at one blow!—that is my way," was the tailor's answer.

So, taking a rope and an axe with him, he went out into the wood, and told those who were ordered to attend him to wait outside. He had not far to seek, the unicorn soon came out and sprang at him, as if he would make an end of him without delay. "Softly, softly," said he, "most haste, worst speed," and remained standing until the animal came quite near, then he slipped quietly behind a tree. The unicorn ran with all his might against the tree and stuck his horn so deep into the trunk that he could not get it out again, and so was taken.

"Now I have you," said the tailor, coming out from behind the tree, and, putting the rope round the unicorn's neck, he took the axe, set free the horn, and when all his party were assembled he led forth the animal and brought it to the King.

The King did not yet wish to give him the promised reward, and set him a third task to do. Before the wedding could take place the tailor was to secure a wild boar which had done a great deal of damage in the wood.

The huntsmen were to accompany him.

"All right," said the tailor, "this is child's play."

But he did not take the huntsmen into the wood, and they were all the better pleased, for the wild boar had many a time before received them in such a way that they had no fancy to disturb him. When the boar caught sight of the tailor he ran at him with foaming mouth and gleaming tusks to bear him to the ground, but the nimble hero rushed into a chapel which chanced to be near, and jumped quickly out of a window on the other side. The boar ran after him, and when he got inside the door shut after him, and there he was imprisoned, for the creature was too big and unwieldly to jump out of the window too. Then the little tailor called the huntsmen that they might see the prisoner with their own eyes; and then he betook himself to the king, who now, whether he liked it or not, was obliged to fulfil his promise, and give him his daughter and the half of his kingdom. But if he had known that the great warrior was only a little tailor he would have taken it still more to heart. So the wedding was celebrated with great splendour and little joy, and the tailor was made into a king.

One night the young queen heard her husband talking in his sleep and saying,

"Now boy, make me that waistcoat and patch me those breeches, or I will lay my yard measure about your shoulders!"

And so, as she perceived of what low birth her husband was, she went to her father the next morning and told him all, and begged him to set her free from a man who was nothing better than a tailor. The king bade her be comforted, saying,

"Tonight, leave your bedroom door open, my guard shall stand outside, and when he is asleep they shall come in and bind him and carry him off to a ship, and he shall be sent to the other side of the world."

So the wife felt consoled, but the king's water-bearer, who had been listening all the while, went to the little tailor and disclosed to him the whole plan.

"I shall put a stop to all this," said he.

At night he lay down as usual in bed, and when his wife thought that he was asleep, she got up, opened the door and lay down again. The little tailor, who only made believe to be asleep, began to murmur plainly,

"Now, boy, make me that waistcoat and patch me those breeches, or I will lay my yard measure about your shoulders! I have slain seven at one blow, killed two giants, caught a unicorn, and taken a wild boar, and shall I be afraid of those who are standing outside my room door?"

And when they heard the tailor say this, a great fear seized them; they fled away as if they had been wild hares, and none of them would venture to attack him.

And so the little tailor all his lifetime remained a king.

Doctor Know-all

ONCE UPON A time a poor Peasant, named Crabb, was taking a load of wood drawn by two oxen to the town for sale. He sold it to a Doctor for four coins. When the money was being paid to him, it so happened that the Doctor was sitting at dinner. When the Peasant saw how daintily the Doctor was eating and drinking, he felt a great desire to become a Doctor too. He remained standing and looking on for a time, and then asked if he could not be a Doctor.

"Oh yes!" said the Doctor; "that is easily managed."

"What must I do?" asked the Peasant.

"First buy an ABC book; you can get one with a cock as a frontispiece. Secondly, turn your wagon and oxen into money, and buy with it clothes and other things suitable for a Doctor. Thirdly, have a sign painted with the words, 'I am Doctor Know-all,' and have it nailed over your door."

The Peasant did everything that he was told to do.

Now when he had been doctoring for a while, not very long though, a rich nobleman had some money stolen from him. He was told about Doctor Know-all, who lived in such and such a village, who would be sure to know what had become of it. So the gentleman ordered his carriage and drove to the village.

He stopped at the Doctor's house, and asked Crabb if he were Doctor Know-all.

"Yes, I am."

"Then you must go with me to get my stolen money back."

"Yes, certainly; but Grethe, my wife, must come too."

The nobleman agreed, and gave both of them seats in his carriage, and they all drove off together.

When they reached the nobleman's castle the dinner was ready, and Crabb was invited to sit down to table.

"Yes; but Grethe, my wife, must dine too"; and he seated himself with her.

When the first Servant brought in a dish of choice food, the Peasant nudged his wife, and said: "Grethe, that was the first,"—meaning that the servant was handing the first dish. But the servant thought he meant, "That was the first thief." As he really was the thief, he became much alarmed, and said to his comrades outside—

"That Doctor knows everything, we shan't get out of this hole; he said I was the first."

The second Servant did not want to go in at all, but he had to go, and when he offered his dish to the Peasant he nudged his wife, and said—"Grethe, that is the second."

This Servant also was frightened and hurried out.

The third one fared no better. The Peasant said again: "Grethe, that is the third."

The fourth one brought in a covered dish, and the master told the Doctor that he must show his powers and guess what was under the cover. Now it was a dish of crabs.

The Peasant looked at the dish and did not know what to do, so he said: 'Wretched Crabb that I am.'

When the Master heard him he cried: "There, he knows it! Then he knows where the money is too."

Then the Servant grew terribly frightened, and signed to the Doctor to come outside.

When he went out, they all four confessed to him that they had stolen the money; they would gladly give it to him and a large sum in addition, if only he would not betray them to their Master, or their necks would be in peril. They also showed him where the money was hidden. Then the Doctor was satisfied, went back to the table, and said—

"Now, Sir, I will look in my book to see where the money is hidden."

The fifth, in the meantime, had crept into the stove to hear if the Doctor knew still more. But he sat there turning over the pages of his ABC book looking for the cock, and as he could not find it at once, he said: "I know you are there, and out you must come."

The man in the stove thought it was meant for him, and sprang out in a fright, crying: "The man knows everything."

Then Doctor Know-all showed the nobleman where the money was hidden, but he did not betray the servants; and he received much money from both sides as a reward, and became a very celebrated man.

The Seven Ravens

THERE WAS ONCE a Man who had seven sons, but never a daughter, however much he wished for one.

At last, however, he had a daughter.

His joy was great, but the child was small and delicate, and, on account of its weakness, it was to be christened at home.

The Father sent one of his sons in haste to the spring to fetch some water; the other six ran with him, and because each of them wanted to be the first to draw the water, between them the pitcher fell into the brook.

There they stood and didn't know what to do, and not one of them ventured to go home.

As they did not come back, their Father became impatient, and said: "Perhaps the young rascals are playing about, and have forgotten it altogether."

He became anxious lest his little girl should die unbaptized, and in hot vexation, he cried: "I wish the youngsters would all turn into Ravens!"

Scarcely were the words uttered, when he heard a whirring in the air above his head, and, looking upwards, he saw seven coal-black Ravens flying away.

The parents could not undo the spell, and were very sad about the loss of their seven sons, but they consoled themselves in some measure with their dear little daughter, who soon became strong, and every day more beautiful.

For a long time she was unaware that she had had any brothers, for her parents took care not to mention it.

However, one day by chance she heard some people saying about her: "Oh yes, the girl's pretty enough; but you know she is really to blame for the misfortune to her seven brothers."

Then she became very sad, and went to her father and mother and asked if she had ever had any brothers, and what had become of them.

The parents could no longer conceal the secret. They said, however, that what had happened was by the decree of heaven, and that her birth was merely the innocent occasion.

But the little girl could not get the matter off her conscience for a single day, and thought that she was bound to release her brothers again. She had no peace or quiet until she had secretly set out, and gone forth into the wide world to trace her brothers, wherever they might be, and to free them, let it cost what it might.

She took nothing with her but a little ring as a remembrance of her parents, a loaf of bread against hunger, a pitcher of water against thirst, and a little chair in case of fatigue. She kept ever going on and on until she came to the end of the world.

Then she came to the Sun, but it was hot and terrible; it devoured little children. She ran hastily away to the Moon, but it was too cold, and, moreover, dismal and dreary. And when the child was looking at it, it said: "I smell, I smell man's flesh!"

Then she quickly made off, and came to the Stars, and they were kind and good, and every one sat on his own special seat.

But the Morning Star stood up, and gave her a little bone, and said: "Unless you have this bone, you cannot open the glass mountain, and in the glass mountain are your brothers."

The girl took the bone, and wrapped it up carefully in a little kerchief, and went on again until she came to the glass mountain.

The gate was closed, and she meant to get out the little

bone. She undid the kerchief and took out the key to open the glass mountain. Then she fitted it into the keyhole, and succeeded in opening the lock.

When she had entered, she met a Dwarf, who said: "My child, what are you looking for?"

"I am looking for my brothers, the Seven Ravens," she answered.

The Dwarf said: "My masters, the Ravens, are not at home; but if you like to wait until they come, please to walk in."

Thereupon the Dwarf brought in the Ravens' supper, on seven little plates, and in seven little cups, and the little sister ate a crumb or two from each of the little plates, and a sip from each of the little cups, but she let the ring she had brought with her fall into the last little cup.

All at once a whirring and crying were heard in the air; then the Dwarf said: "Now my masters the Ravens are coming home."

Then they came in, and wanted to eat and drink, and began to look about for their little plates and cups.

But they said one after another: "Halloa! who has been eating off my plate? Who has been drinking out of my cup? There has been some human mouth here."

And when the seventh drank to the bottom of his cup, the ring rolled up against his lips.

He looked at it, and recognised it as a ring belonging to his father and mother, and said: "God grant that our sister may be here, and that we may be delivered."

As the maiden was standing behind the door listening, she heard the wish and came forward, and then all the Ravens got back their human form again.

And they embraced and kissed one another, and went joyfully home.

The Elves and the Shoemaker

THERE WAS ONCE a shoemaker, who, through no fault of his own, became so poor that at last he had nothing left but just enough leather to make one pair of shoes. He cut out the shoes at night, so as to set to work upon them next morning; and as he had a good conscience, he laid himself quietly down in his bed, committed himself to heaven, and fell asleep. In the morning, after he had said his prayers, and was going to get to work, he found the pair of shoes made and finished, and standing on his table. He was very much astonished, and could not tell what to think, and he took the shoes in his hand to examine them more nearly; and they were so well made that every stitch was in its right place, just as if they had come from the hand of a master-workman.

Soon after a purchaser entered, and as the shoes fitted him very well, he gave more than the usual price for them, so that the shoemaker had enough money to buy leather for two more pairs of shoes. He cut them out at night, and intended to set to work the next morning with fresh spirit; but that was not to be, for when he got up they were already finished, and a customer even was not lacking, who gave him so much money that he was able to buy leather enough for four new pairs. Early next morning he found the four pairs also finished, and so it always happened; whatever he cut out in the evening was worked up by the morning, so that he was soon in the way of making a good living, and in the end became very well to do.

One night, not long before Christmas, when the shoe-maker had finished cutting out, and before he went to bed, he said to his wife,

"How would it be if we were to sit up tonight and see who it is that does us this service?"

His wife agreed, and set a light to burn. Then they both hid in a corner of the room, behind some coats that were hanging up, and then they began to watch. As soon as it was midnight they saw come in two neatly-formed naked little men, who seated themselves at the shoemaker's table, and took up the work that was already prepared, and began to stitch, to pierce, and to hammer so cleverly and quickly with their little fingers that the shoemaker's eyes could scarcely follow them, so full of wonder was he. And they never left off until everything was finished and was standing ready on the table, and then they jumped up and ran off.

The next morning the shoemaker's wife said to her hus-band, "Those little men have made us rich, and we ought to show ourselves grateful. With all their running about, and having nothing to cover them, they must be very cold. I'll tell you what; I will make them little shirts, coats, waistcoats, and breeches for them, and knit each of them a pair of stockings, and you shall make each of them a pair of shoes."

The husband consented willingly, and at night, when everything was finished, they laid the gifts together on the table, instead of the cut-out work, and placed themselves so that they could observe how the little men would behave. When midnight came, they rushed in, ready to set to work, but when they found, instead of the pieces of pre-pared leather, the neat little garments put ready for them, they stood a moment in surprise, and then they testified the greatest delight. With the greatest swiftness they took up the pretty garments and slipped them on, singing,

> "What spruce and dandy boys are we!
> No longer cobblers we will be."

Then they hopped and danced about, jumping over the chairs and tables, and at last they danced out at the door.

From that time they were never seen again; but it always went well with the shoemaker as long as he lived, and whatever he took in hand prospered.

The Lady and the Lion

THERE WAS ONCE a Man who had to take a long journey, and when he was saying good-bye to his daughters he asked what he should bring back to them.

The eldest wanted pearls, the second diamonds, but
the third said, "Dear father, I should like a singing, soaring
lark."

The father said, "Very well, if I can manage it, you shall
have it"; and he kissed all three and set off. He bought
pearls and diamonds for the two eldest, but he had
searched everywhere in vain for the singing, soaring lark,
and this worried him, for his youngest daughter was his
favourite child.

Once his way led through a wood, in the midst of which
was a splendid castle; near it stood a tree, and right up at
the top he saw a lark singing and soaring. "Ah," he said, "I
have come across you in the nick of time"; and he called
to his Servant to dismount and catch the little creature.
But as he approached the tree a Lion sprang out from
underneath, and shook himself, and roared so that the
leaves on the tree trembled.

"Who dares to steal my lark?" said he. "I will eat up the
thief!"

Then the Man said, "I didn't know that the bird was
yours. I will make up for my fault by paying a heavy ran-
som. Only spare my life."

But the Lion said, "Nothing can save you, unless you
promise to give me whatever first meets you when you get

home. If you consent, I will give you your life and the bird into the bargain."

But the Man hesitated, and said, "Suppose my youngest and favourite daughter were to come running to meet me when I go home!"

But the Servant was afraid, and said, "Your daughter will not necessarily be the first to come to meet you; it might just as well be a cat or a dog."

So the Man let himself be persuaded, took the lark, and promised to the Lion for his own whatever first met him on his return home. When he reached home, and entered his house, the first person who met him was none other than his youngest daughter; she came running up and kissed and caressed him, and when she saw that he had brought the singing, soaring lark, she was beside herself with joy. But her father could not rejoice; he began to cry, and said, "My dear child, it has cost me dear, for I have had to promise you to a Lion who will tear you in pieces when he has you in his power." And he told her all that had happened, and begged her not to go, come what might.

But she consoled him, saying, "Dear father, what you have promised must be performed. I will go and will soon soften the Lion's heart, so that I shall come back safe and sound." The next morning the way was shown to her, and she said good-bye and went confidently into the forest.

Now the Lion was an enchanted Prince, who was a Lion by day, and all his followers were Lions too; but by night they reassumed their human form. On her arrival she was kindly received, and conducted to the castle. When night fell, the Lion turned into a handsome man, and their wedding was celebrated with due magnificence. And they lived happily together, sitting up at night and sleeping by day. One day he came to her and said, "Tomorrow there is a festival at your father's house to celebrate your eldest sister's wedding; if you would like to go my Lions shall escort you."

She answered that she was very eager to see her father again, so she went away accompanied by the Lions.

There was great rejoicing on her coming, for they all thought that she had been torn to pieces and had long been dead.

But she told them what a handsome husband she had and how well she fared; and she stayed with them as long as the wedding festivities lasted. Then she went back again into the wood.

When the second daughter married, and the youngest was again invited to the wedding, she said to the Lion, "This time I will not go alone, you must come too."

But the Lion said it would be too dangerous, for if a gleam of light touched him he would be changed into a Dove and would have to fly about for seven years.

"Ah," said she, "only go with me, and I will protect you and keep off every ray of light."

So they went away together, and took their little child with them too. They had a hall built with such thick walls that no ray could penetrate, and thither the Lion was to retire when the wedding torches were kindled. But the door was made of fresh wood which split and caused a little crack which no one noticed.

Now the wedding was celebrated with great splendour. But when the procession came back from church with a large number of torches and lights, a ray of light no broader than a hair fell upon the Prince, and the minute this ray touched him he was changed; and when his wife came in and looked for him, she saw nothing but a White Dove sitting there. The Dove said to her, "For seven years I must fly about the world; every seventh step I will let fall a drop of blood and a white feather which will show you the way, and if you will follow the track you can free me."

Thereupon the Dove flew out of the door, and she followed it, and every seventh step it let fall a drop of blood and a little white feather to show her the way. So she wandered about the world, and never rested till the seven years were nearly passed. Then she rejoiced, thinking that she would soon be free of her troubles; but she was still far from release. One day as they were journeying on in the accustomed way, the feather and the drop of blood ceased falling, and when she looked up the Dove had vanished.

"Man cannot help me," she thought. So she climbed up to the Sun and said to it, "You shine upon all the valleys and mountain peaks, have you not seen a White Dove flying by?"

"No," said the Sun, "I have not seen one; but I will give you a little casket. Open it when you are in dire need."

She thanked the Sun, and went on till night, when the Moon shone out. "You shine all night," she said, "over field and forest, have you seen a White Dove flying by?"

"No," answered the Moon, "I have seen none; but here is an egg. Break it when you are in great need."

She thanked the Moon, and went on till the Night Wind blew upon her. "You blow among all the trees and leaves, have not you seen a White Dove?" she asked.

"No," said the Night Wind, "I have not seen one; but I will ask the other three Winds, who may, perhaps, have seen it."

The East Wind and the West Wind came, but they had seen no Dove. Only the South Wind said, "I have seen the White Dove. It has flown away to the Red Sea, where it has again become a Lion, since the seven years are over; and the Lion is ever fighting with a Dragon who is an enchanted Princess."

Then the Night Wind said, "I will advise you. Go to the Red Sea, you will find tall reeds growing on the right bank; count them, and cut down the eleventh, strike the Dragon with it and then the Lion will be able to master it, and both will regain human shape. Next, look round, and you will see the winged Griffin, who dwells by the Red Sea, leap upon its back with your beloved, and it will carry you across the sea. Here is a nut. Drop it when you come to mid-ocean; it will open immediately and a tall nut tree will grow up out of the water, on which the Griffin will settle. Could it not rest, it would not be strong enough to carry you across, and if you forget to drop the nut, it will let you fall into the sea."

Then she journeyed on, and found everything as the Night Wind had said. She counted the reeds by the sea and cut off the eleventh, struck the Dragon with it, and the Lion mastered it; immediately both regained human form. But when the Princess who had been a Dragon was free from enchantment, she took the Prince in her arms, seated herself on the Griffin's back, and carried him off. And the poor wanderer, again forsaken, sat down and cried. At last she took courage and said to herself: "Wherever the winds blow, I will go, and as long as cocks crow, I will search till I find him."

So she went on a long, long way, till she came to the castle where the Prince and Princess were living. There she heard that there was to be a festival to celebrate their wedding. Then she said to herself, "Heaven help me," and she opened the casket which the Sun had given her; inside it was a dress, as brilliant as the Sun itself. She took it out, put it on, and went into the castle, where every one, including the Bride, looked at her with amazement. The dress pleased the Bride so much that she asked if it was to be bought.

"Not with gold or goods," she answered; "but with flesh and blood."

The Bride asked what she meant, and she answered, "Let me speak with the Bridegroom in his chamber tonight."

The Bride refused. However, she wanted the dress so much that at last she consented; but the Chamberlain was ordered to give the Prince a sleeping draught.

At night, when the Prince was asleep, she was taken to his room. She sat down and said: "For seven years I have followed you. I have been to the Sun, and the Moon, and the Four Winds to look for you. I have helped you against the Dragon, and will you now quite forget me?"

But the Prince slept so soundly that he thought it was only the rustling of the wind among the pine trees. When morning came she was taken away, and had to give up the dress; and as it had not helped her she was very sad, and went out into a meadow and cried. As she was sitting there, she remembered the egg which the Moon had given her; she broke it open, and out came a hen and twelve chickens, all of gold, who ran about chirping, and then crept back under their mother's wings. A prettier sight could not be seen. She got up and drove them about the meadow, till the Bride saw them from the window. The chickens pleased her so much that she asked if they were for sale. "Not for gold and goods, but for flesh and blood. Let me speak with the Bridegroom in his chamber once more."

The Bride said "Yes," intending to deceive her as before; but when the Prince went to his room he asked the Chamberlain what all the murmuring and rustling in the night meant. Then the Chamberlain told him how he had been ordered to give him a sleeping draught because a poor girl had been concealed in his room, and that night he was to do the same again. "Pour out the drink, and put it near my bed," said the Prince. At night she was brought in again, and when she began to relate her sad fortunes he recognised the voice of his dear wife, sprang up, and said, "Now I am really free for the first time. All has been as a dream, for the foreign Princess cast a spell over me so that I was forced to forget you; but heaven in a happy hour has taken away my blindness."

Then they both stole out of the castle, for they feared the Princess's father, because he was a sorcerer. They mounted the Griffin, who bore them over the Red Sea, and when they got to mid-ocean, she dropped the nut. On the spot a fine nut tree sprang up, on which the bird rested; then it took them home, where they found their child grown tall and beautiful, and they lived happily till the end.

The Goose Girl

THERE LIVED ONCE an old Queen, whose husband had been dead many years. She had a beautiful daughter who was promised in marriage to a King's son living a great way off. When the time appointed for the wedding drew near, and the old Queen had to send her daughter into the foreign land, she got together many costly things, furniture and cups and jewels and adornments, both of gold and silver, everything proper for the dowry of a royal Princess, for she loved her daughter dearly. She gave her also a waiting gentlewoman to attend her and to give her into the bridegroom's hands; and they were each to have a horse for the journey, and the Princess's horse was named Falada, and he could speak. When the time for parting came, the old Queen took her daughter to her chamber, and with a little knife she cut her own finger so that it bled; and she held beneath it a white napkin, and on it fell three drops of blood; and she gave it to her daughter, bidding her take care of it, for it would be needful to her on the way. Then they took leave of each other; and the Princess put the napkin in her bosom, got on her horse, and set out to go to the bridegroom. After she had ridden an hour, she began to feel very thirsty, and she said to the waiting woman,

"Get down, and fill my cup that you are carrying with water from the brook; I have great desire to drink."

"Get down yourself," said the waiting woman, "and if you are thirsty stoop down and drink; I will not be your slave."

And as her thirst was so great, the Princess had to get down and to stoop and drink of the water of the brook, and could not have her gold cup to serve her. "Oh dear!" said the poor Princess. And the three drops of blood heard her, and said,

"If your mother knew of this, it would break her heart."

But the Princess answered nothing, and quietly mounted her horse again. So they rode on some miles farther; the day was warm, the sun shone hot, and the Princess grew thirsty once more. And when they came to a water-course she called again to the waiting woman and said,

"Get down, and give me to drink out of my golden cup." For she had forgotten all that had gone before. But the waiting woman spoke still more scornfully and said,

"If you want a drink, you may get it yourself; I am not going to be your slave."

So, as her thirst was so great, the Princess had to get off her horse and to stoop towards the running water to drink, and as she stooped, she wept and said, "Oh dear!" And the three drops of blood heard her and answered,

"If your mother knew of this, it would break her heart!"

And as she drank and stooped over, the napkin on which were the three drops of blood fell out of her bosom and floated down the stream, and in her distress she never noticed it; not so the waiting woman, who rejoiced because she should have power over the bride, who, now that she had lost the three drops of blood, had become weak, and unable to defend herself. And when she was going to mount her horse again the waiting woman cried,

"Falada belongs to me, and this jade to you." And the Princess had to give way and let it be as she said. Then the waiting woman ordered the Princess with many hard words to take off her rich clothing and to put on her plain garments, and then she made her swear to say nothing of the matter when they came to the royal court; threatening to take her life if she refused. And all the while Falada noticed and remembered.

The waiting woman then mounting Falada, and the

Princess the sorry jade, they journeyed on till they reached the royal castle. There was great joy at their coming, and the King's son hastened to meet them, and lifted the waiting woman from her horse, thinking she was his bride; and then he led her up the stairs, while the real Princess had to remain below. But the old King, who was looking out of the window, saw her standing in the yard, and noticed how delicate and gentle and beautiful she was, and then he went down and asked the seeming bride who it was that she had brought with her and that was now standing in the courtyard.

"Oh!" answered the bride, "I only brought her with me for company; give the maid something to do, that she may not be for ever standing idle."

But the old King had no work to give her; until he bethought him of a boy he had who took care of the geese, and that she might help him. And so the real Princess was sent to keep geese with the goose boy, who was called Conrad.

Soon after the false bride said to the Prince,

"Dearest husband, I pray thee do me a pleasure."

"With all my heart," answered he.

"Then," said she, "send for the knacker, that he may carry off the horse I came here upon, and make away with him; he was very troublesome to me on the journey." For she was afraid that the horse might tell how she had behaved to the Princess. And when the order had been given that Falada should die, it came to the Princess's ears, and she came to the knacker's man secretly, and promised him a piece of gold if he would do her a service. There was in the town a great dark gateway through which she had to pass morning and evening with her geese, and she asked the man to take Falada's head and to nail it on the gate, that she might always see it as she passed by. And the man promised, and he took Falada's head and nailed it fast in the dark gateway.

Early next morning as she and Conrad drove their geese through the gate, she said as she went by,

"O Falada, dost thou hang there?"

And the head answered,

> "Princess, dost thou so meanly fare?
> But if thy mother knew thy pain,
> Her heart would surely break in twain."

But she went on through the town, driving her geese to the field. And when they came into the meadows, she sat down and undid her hair, which was all of gold, and when Conrad saw how it glistened, he wanted to pull out a few hairs for himself. And she said,

> "O wind, blow Conrad's hat away,
> Make him run after as it flies,
> While I with my gold hair will play,
> And twist it up in seemly wise."

Then there came a wind strong enough to blow Conrad's hat far away over the fields, and he had to run after it; and by the time he came back she had put up her hair with combs and pins, and he could not get at any to pull it out; and he was sulky and would not speak to her; so they looked after the geese until the evening came, and then they went home.

The next morning, as they passed under the dark gateway, the Princess said,

> "O Falada, dost thou hang there?"

And Falada answered,

> "Princess, dost thou so meanly fare?
> But if thy mother knew thy pain,
> Her heart would surely break in twain."

And when they reached the fields she sat down and

began to comb out her hair; then Conrad came up and wanted to seize upon some of it, and she cried,

> "O wind, blow Conrad's hat away,
>   Make him run after as it flies,
>   While I with my gold hair will play,
>   And do it up in seemly wise."

Then the wind came and blew Conrad's hat very far away, so that he had to run after it, and when he came back again her hair was put up again, so that he could pull none of it out; and they tended the geese until the evening.

And after they had got home, Conrad went to the old King and said, "I will tend the geese no longer with that girl!"

"Why not?" asked the Old King.

"Because she vexes me the whole day long," answered Conrad. Then the old King ordered him to tell how it was.

"Every morning," said Conrad, "as we pass under the dark gateway with the geese, there is an old horse's head hanging on the wall, and she says to it,

> "O Falada, dost thou hang there?"

And the head answers,

> "Princess, dost thou so meanly fare?
>   But if thy mother knew thy pain,
>   Her heart would surely break in twain."

And besides this, Conrad related all that happened in the fields, and how he was obliged to run after his hat.

The old King told him to go to drive the geese next morning as usual, and he himself went behind the gate and listened how the maiden spoke to Falada; and then he followed them into the fields, and hid himself behind a bush; and he watched the goose boy and the goose girl

tend the geese; and after a while he saw the girl make her
hair all loose, and how it gleamed and shone. Soon she
said,

> "O wind, blow Conrad's hat away,
> And make him follow as it flies,
> While I with my gold hair will play,
> And bind it up in seemly wise."

Then there came a gust of wind and away went Conrad's hat, and he after it, while the maiden combed and
bound up her hair; and the old King saw all that went on.
At last he went unnoticed away, and when the goose girl
came back in the evening he sent for her, and asked the
reason of her doing all this.

"That I dare not tell you," she answered, "nor can I tell
any man of my woe, for when I was in danger of my life I
swore an oath not to reveal it." And he pressed her sore,
and left her no peace, but he could get nothing out of her.
At last he said,

"If you will not tell it me, tell it to the iron oven," and
went away. Then she crept into the iron oven, and began
to weep and to lament, and at last she opened her heart
and said,

"Here I sit forsaken of all the world, and I am a King's
daughter, and a wicked waiting woman forced me to give
up my royal garments and my place at the bridegroom's
side, and I am made a goose girl, and have to do mean service. And if my mother knew, it would break her heart."

Now the old King was standing outside by the oven door
listening, and he heard all she said, and he called to her
and told her to come out of the oven. And he caused royal
clothing to be put upon her, and it was a marvel to see how
beautiful she was. The old King then called his son and
proved to him that he had the wrong bride, for she was
really only a waiting woman, and that the true bride was
here at hand, she who had been the goose girl. The Prince
was glad at heart when he saw her beauty and gentleness;

and a great feast was made ready, and all the court people and good friends were bidden to it. The bridegroom sat in the midst with the Princess on one side and the waiting woman on the other; and the false bride did not know the true one, because she was dazzled with her glittering braveries. When all the company had eaten and drunk and were merry, the old King gave the waiting woman a question to answer, as to what such an one deserved, who had deceived her masters in such and such a manner, telling the whole story, and ending by asking,

"Now, what doom does such an one deserve?"

"No better than this," answered the false bride, "that she be put naked into a cask, studded inside with sharp nails, and be dragged along in it by two white horses from street to street, until she be dead."

"Thou hast spoken thy own doom," said the old King; "as thou hast said, so shall it be done." And when the sentence was fulfilled, the Prince married the true bride, and ever after they ruled over their kingdom in peace and blessedness.

Jorinda and Joringel

THERE WAS ONCE an old castle in the middle of a vast thick wood; in it there lived an old woman quite alone, and she was a witch. By day she made herself into a cat or a screech-owl, but regularly at night she became a human being again. In this way she was able to decoy wild beasts and birds, which she would kill, and boil or roast. If any man came within a hundred paces of the castle, he was forced to stand still and could not move from the place till she gave the word of release; but if an innocent maiden came within the circle she changed her into a bird, and shut her up in a cage which she carried into a room in the castle. She must have had seven thousand cages of this kind, containing pretty birds.

Now, there was once a maiden called Jorinda who was more beautiful than all other maidens. She had promised to marry a very handsome youth named Joringel, and it was in the days of their courtship, when they took the greatest joy in being alone together, that one day they wandered out into the forest. "Take care," said Joringel; "do not let us go too near the castle."

It was a lovely evening. The sunshine glanced between the tree trunks of the dark green wood, while the turtle-doves sang plaintively in the old beech trees. Yet Jorinda sat down in the sunshine, and could not help weeping and bewailing, while Joringel, too, soon became just as mournful. They both felt as miserable as if they had been going to die. Gazing round them, they found they had lost their

way, and did not know how they should find the path
home. Half the sun still appeared above the mountain;
half had sunk below. Joringel peered into the bushes and
saw the old walls of the castle quite close to them; he was
terror-struck, and became pale as death. Jorinda was
singing:

> "My birdie with its ring so red,
>   Sings sorrow, sorrow, sorrow;
> My love will mourn when I am dead,
>   Tomorrow, morrow, mor——jug, jug."

Joringel looked at her, but she was changed into a
nightingale who sang "Jug, Jug."

A screech-owl with glowing eyes flew three times round
her, and cried three times "Shu hu-hu." Joringel could not
stir; he stood like a stone without being able to speak, or
cry, or move hand or foot. The sun had now set; the owl
flew into a bush, out of which appeared almost at the
same moment a crooked old woman, skinny and yellow;
she had big, red eyes and a crooked nose whose tip
reached her chin. She mumbled something, caught the
nightingale, and carried it away in her hand. Joringel
could not say a word nor move from the spot, and the
nightingale was gone. At last the old woman came back,
and said in a droning voice: "Greeting to thee, Zachiel!
When the moon shines upon the cage, unloose the cap-
tive, Zachiel!"

Then Joringel was free. He fell on his knees before the
witch, and implored her to give back his Jorinda; but she
said he should never have her again, and went away. He
pleaded, he wept, he lamented, but all in vain. "Alas! what
is to become of me?" said Joringel. At last he went away,
and arrived at a strange village, where he spent a long
time as a shepherd. He often wandered round about the
castle, but did not go too near it. At last he dreamt one
night that he found a blood-red flower, in the midst of
which was a beautiful large pearl. He plucked the flower,

and took it to the castle. Whatever he touched with it was made free of enchantment. He dreamt, too, that by this means he had found his Jorinda again. In the morning when he awoke he began to search over hill and dale, in the hope of finding a flower like this; he searched till the ninth day, when he found the flower early in the morning. In the middle was a big dewdrop, as big as the finest pearl. This flower he carried day and night, till he reached the castle. He was not held fast as before when he came within the hundred paces of the castle, but walked straight up to the door.

Joringel was filled with joy; he touched the door with the flower, and it flew open. He went in through the court, and listened for the sound of birds. He went on, and found the hall, where the witch was feeding the birds in the seven thousand cages. When she saw Joringel she was angry, very angry—scolded, and spat poison, and gall at him. He paid no attention to her, but turned away and searched among the bird-cages. Yes, but there were many hundred nightingales; how was he to find his Jorinda?

While he was looking about in this way he noticed that the old woman was secretly removing a cage with a bird inside, and was making for the door. He sprang swiftly towards her, touched the cage and the witch with the flower, and then she no longer had power to exercise her spells. Jorinda stood there, as beautiful as before, and threw her arms round Joringel's neck. After that he changed all the other birds back into maidens again, and went home with Jorinda, and they lived long and happily together.

The Twelve Dancing Princesses

THERE WAS ONCE a King who had twelve daughters, each more beautiful than the other. They slept together in a hall where their beds stood close to one another; and at night, when they had gone to bed, the King locked the door and bolted it. But when he unlocked it in the morning, he noticed that their shoes had been danced to pieces, and nobody could explain how it happened. So the King sent out a proclamation saying that any one who could discover where the Princesses did their night's dancing should choose one of them to be his wife and should reign after his death; but whoever presented himself, and failed to make the discovery after three days and nights, was to forfeit his life.

A Prince soon presented himself and offered to take the risk. He was well received, and at night was taken into a room adjoining the hall where the Princesses slept. His bed was made up there, and he was to watch and see where they went to dance; so that they could not do anything, or go anywhere else, the door of his room was left open too. But the eyes of the Prince grew heavy, and he fell asleep. When he woke up in the morning all the twelve had been dancing, for the soles of their shoes were full of holes. The second and third evenings passed with the same results, and then the Prince found no mercy, and his head was cut off. Many others came after him and offered to take the risk, but they all had to lose their lives.

Now it happened that a poor Soldier, who had been

wounded and could no longer serve, found himself on the road to the town where the King lived. There he fell in with an old woman who asked him where he intended to go.

"I really don't know, myself," he said; and added, in fun, "I should like to discover where the King's daughters dance their shoes into holes, and after that to become King."

"That is not so difficult," said the old woman. "You must not drink the wine which will be brought to you in the evening, but must pretend to be fast asleep." Whereupon she gave him a short cloak, saying: "When you wear this you will be invisible, and then you can slip out after the Twelve Princesses."

As soon as the Soldier heard this good advice he took it up seriously, plucked up courage, appeared before the King, and offered himself as suitor. He was as well received as the others, and was dressed in royal garments.

In the evening, when bedtime came, he was conducted to the anteroom. As he was about to go to bed the eldest Princess appeared, bringing him a cup of wine; but he had fastened a sponge under his chin and let the wine run down into it, so that he did not drink one drop. Then he lay down, and when he had been quite a little while he began to snore as though in the deepest sleep.

The Twelve Princesses heard him, and laughed. The eldest said: "He, too, must forfeit his life."

Then they got up, opened cupboards, chests, and cases, and brought out their beautiful dresses. They decked themselves before the glass, skipping about and revelling in the prospect of the dance. Only the youngest sister said: "I don't know what it is. You may rejoice, but I feel so strange; a misfortune is certainly hanging over us."

"You are a little goose," answered the eldest; "you are always frightened. Have you forgotten how many Princes have come here in vain? Why, I need not have given the Soldier a sleeping draught at all; the blockhead would never have awakened."

When they were all ready they looked at the Soldier; but his eyes were shut and he did not stir. So they thought they would soon be quite safe. Then the eldest went up to one of the beds and knocked on it; it sank into the earth, and they descended through the opening, one after another, the eldest first.

The Soldier, who had noticed everything, did not hesitate long, but threw on his cloak and went down behind the youngest. Half-way down he trod on her dress. She was frightened, and said: "What was that? Who is holding on to my dress?"

"Don't be so foolish. You must have caught on a nail," said the eldest. Then they went right down, and when they got quite underground, they stood in a marvellously beautiful avenue of trees; all the leaves were silver, and glittered and shone.

The Soldier thought, "I must take away some token with me." And as he broke off a twig, a sharp crack came from the tree.

The youngest cried out, "All is not well; did you hear that sound?"

"Those are triumphal salutes, because we shall soon have released our Princes," said the eldest.

Next day they came to an avenue where all the leaves were of gold, and, at last, into a third, where they were of shining diamonds. From both these he broke off a twig, and there was a crack each time which made the youngest Princess start with terror; but the eldest maintained that the sounds were only triumphal salutes. They went on faster, and came to a great lake. Close to the bank lay twelve little boats, and in every boat sat a handsome Prince. They had expected the Twelve Princesses, and each took one with him; but the Soldier seated himself by the youngest.

Then said the Prince, "I don't know why, but the boat is much heavier today, and I am obliged to row with all my strength to get it along."

"I wonder why it is," said the youngest, "unless, per-haps, it is the hot weather; it is strangely hot."

On the opposite side of the lake stood a splendid brightly-lighted castle, from which came the sound of the joyous music of trumpets and drums. They rowed across, and every Prince danced with his love; and the Soldier danced too, unseen. If one of the Princesses held a cup of wine he drank out of it, so that it was empty when she lifted it to her lips. This frightened the youngest one, but the eldest always silenced her. They danced till three next morning, when their shoes were danced into holes, and they were obliged to stop. The Princes took them back across the lake, and this time the Soldier took his seat beside the eldest. On the bank they said farewell to their Princes, and promised to come again the next night. When they got to the steps, the Soldier ran on ahead, lay down in the bed, and when the twelve came lagging by, slowly and wearily, he began to snore again, very loud, so that they said, "We are quite safe as far as he is concerned." Then they took off their beautiful dresses, put them away, placed the worn-out shoes under their beds, and lay down.

The next morning the Soldier determined to say noth-ing, but to see the wonderful doings again. So he went with them the second and third nights. Everything was just the same as the first time, and they danced each time till their shoes were in holes; but the third time the Sol-dier took away a wine-cup as a token.

When the appointed hour came for his answer, he took the three twigs and the cup with him and went before the King. The Twelve Princesses stood behind the door lis-tening to hear what he would say. When the King put the question, "Where did my daughters dance their shoes to pieces in the night?" he answered: "With twelve Princes in an underground castle." Then he produced the tokens.

The King sent for his daughters and asked them whether the Soldier had spoken the truth. As they saw that they were betrayed, and would gain nothing by lies, they were obliged to admit all. Thereupon the King asked the Soldier which one he would choose as his wife. He answered: "I am no longer young, give me the eldest."

So the wedding was celebrated that very day, and the kingdom was promised to him on the King's death. But for every night which the Princes had spent in dancing with the Princesses a day was added to their time of enchantment.

FICTION

FLATLAND: A ROMANCE OF MANY DIMENSIONS, Edwin A. Abbott. 96pp. 0-486-27263-X

SHORT STORIES, Louisa May Alcott. 64pp. 0-486-29063-8

WINESBURG, OHIO, Sherwood Anderson. 160pp. 0-486-28269-4

PERSUASION, Jane Austen. 224pp. 0-486-29555-9

PRIDE AND PREJUDICE, Jane Austen. 272pp. 0-486-28473-5

SENSE AND SENSIBILITY, Jane Austen. 272pp. 0-486-29049-2

LOOKING BACKWARD, Edward Bellamy. 160pp. 0-486-29038-7

BEOWULF, Beowulf (trans. by R. K. Gordon). 64pp. 0-486-27264-8

CIVIL WAR STORIES, Ambrose Bierce. 128pp. 0-486-28038-1

WUTHERING HEIGHTS, Emily Brontë. 256pp. 0-486-29256-8

THE THIRTY-NINE STEPS, John Buchan. 96pp. 0-486-28201-5

TARZAN OF THE APES, Edgar Rice Burroughs. 224pp. (Not available in Europe or United Kingdom.) 0-486-29570-2

ALICE'S ADVENTURES IN WONDERLAND, Lewis Carroll. 96pp. 0-486-27543-4

THROUGH THE LOOKING-GLASS, Lewis Carroll. 128pp. 0-486-40878-7

MY ÁNTONIA, Willa Cather. 176pp. 0-486-28240-6

O PIONEERS!, Willa Cather. 128pp. 0-486-27785-2

FIVE GREAT SHORT STORIES, Anton Chekhov. 96pp. 0-486-26463-7

TALES OF CONJURE AND THE COLOR LINE, Charles Waddell Chesnutt. 128pp. 0-486-40426-9

FAVORITE FATHER BROWN STORIES, G. K. Chesterton. 96pp. 0-486-27545-0

THE AWAKENING, Kate Chopin. 128pp. 0-486-27786-0

A PAIR OF SILK STOCKINGS AND OTHER STORIES, Kate Chopin. 64pp. 0-486-29264-9

HEART OF DARKNESS, Joseph Conrad. 80pp. 0-486-26464-5

LORD JIM, Joseph Conrad. 256pp. 0-486-40650-4

THE SECRET SHARER AND OTHER STORIES, Joseph Conrad. 128pp. 0-486-27546-9

THE "LITTLE REGIMENT" AND OTHER CIVIL WAR STORIES, Stephen Crane. 80pp. 0-486-29557-5

THE OPEN BOAT AND OTHER STORIES, Stephen Crane. 128pp. 0-486-27547-7

THE RED BADGE OF COURAGE, Stephen Crane. 112pp. 0-486-26465-3

MOLL FLANDERS, Daniel Defoe. 256pp. 0-486-29093-X

ROBINSON CRUSOE, Daniel Defoe. 288pp. 0-486-40427-7

A CHRISTMAS CAROL, Charles Dickens. 80pp. 0-486-26865-9

THE CRICKET ON THE HEARTH AND OTHER CHRISTMAS STORIES, Charles Dickens. 128pp. 0-486-28039-X

A TALE OF TWO CITIES, Charles Dickens. 304pp. 0-486-40651-2

THE DOUBLE, Fyodor Dostoyevsky. 128pp. 0-486-29572-9

THE GAMBLER, Fyodor Dostoyevsky. 112pp. 0-486-29081-6

NOTES FROM THE UNDERGROUND, Fyodor Dostoyevsky. 96pp. 0-486-27053-X

THE ADVENTURE OF THE DANCING MEN AND OTHER STORIES, Sir Arthur Conan Doyle. 80pp. 0-486-29558-3

THE HOUND OF THE BASKERVILLES, Arthur Conan Doyle. 128pp. 0-486-28214-7

THE LOST WORLD, Arthur Conan Doyle. 176pp. 0-486-40060-3

DOVER · THRIFT · EDITIONS

FICTION

A JOURNAL OF THE PLAGUE YEAR, Daniel Defoe. 192pp. 0-486-41919-3
SIX GREAT SHERLOCK HOLMES STORIES, Sir Arthur Conan Doyle. 112pp. 0-486-27055-6
SHORT STORIES, Theodore Dreiser. 112pp. 0-486-28215-5
SILAS MARNER, George Eliot. 160pp. 0-486-29246-0
JOSEPH ANDREWS, Henry Fielding. 288pp. 0-486-41588-0
THIS SIDE OF PARADISE, F. Scott Fitzgerald. 208pp. 0-486-28999-0
"THE DIAMOND AS BIG AS THE RITZ" AND OTHER STORIES, F. Scott Fitzgerald.
    0-486-29991-0
MADAME BOVARY, Gustave Flaubert. 256pp. 0-486-29257-6
THE REVOLT OF "MOTHER" AND OTHER STORIES, Mary E. Wilkins Freeman. 128pp.
    0-486-40428-5
A ROOM WITH A VIEW, E. M. Forster. 176pp. (Available in U.S. only.) 0-486-28467-0
WHERE ANGELS FEAR TO TREAD, E. M. Forster. 128pp. (Available in U.S. only.)
    0-486-27791-7
THE IMMORALIST, André Gide. 112pp. (Available in U.S. only.) 0-486-29237-1
HERLAND, Charlotte Perkins Gilman. 128pp. 0-486-40429-3
"THE YELLOW WALLPAPER" AND OTHER STORIES, Charlotte Perkins Gilman. 80pp.
    0-486-29857-4
THE OVERCOAT AND OTHER STORIES, Nikolai Gogol. 112pp. 0-486-27057-2
CHELKASH AND OTHER STORIES, Maxim Gorky. 64pp. 0-486-40652-0
GREAT GHOST STORIES, John Grafton (ed.). 112pp. 0-486-27270-2
DETECTION BY GASLIGHT, Douglas G. Greene (ed.). 272pp. 0-486-29928-7
THE MABINOGION, Lady Charlotte E. Guest. 192pp. 0-486-29541-9
"THE FIDDLER OF THE REELS" AND OTHER SHORT STORIES, Thomas Hardy. 80pp.
    0-486-29960-6
THE LUCK OF ROARING CAMP AND OTHER STORIES, Bret Harte. 96pp. 0-486-27271-0
THE HOUSE OF THE SEVEN GABLES, Nathaniel Hawthorne. 272pp. 0-486-40882-5
THE SCARLET LETTER, Nathaniel Hawthorne. 192pp. 0-486-28048-9
YOUNG GOODMAN BROWN AND OTHER STORIES, Nathaniel Hawthorne. 128pp.
    0-486-27060-2
THE GIFT OF THE MAGI AND OTHER SHORT STORIES, O. Henry. 96pp. 0-486-27061-0
THE ASPERN PAPERS, Henry James. 112pp. 0-486-41922-3
THE BEAST IN THE JUNGLE AND OTHER STORIES, Henry James. 128pp. 0-486-27552-3
DAISY MILLER, Henry James. 64pp. 0-486-28773-4
THE TURN OF THE SCREW, Henry James. 96pp. 0-486-26684-2
WASHINGTON SQUARE, Henry James. 176pp. 0-486-40431-5
THE COUNTRY OF THE POINTED FIRS, Sarah Orne Jewett. 96pp. 0-486-28196-5
THE AUTOBIOGRAPHY OF AN EX-COLORED MAN, James Weldon Johnson. 112pp.
    0-486-28512-X
DUBLINERS, James Joyce. 160pp. 0-486-26870-5
A PORTRAIT OF THE ARTIST AS A YOUNG MAN, James Joyce. 192pp. 0-486-28050-0
THE METAMORPHOSIS AND OTHER STORIES, Franz Kafka. 96pp. 0-486-29030-1
THE MAN WHO WOULD BE KING AND OTHER STORIES, Rudyard Kipling. 128pp.
    0-486-28051-9
YOU KNOW ME AL, Ring Lardner. 128pp. 0-486-28513-8
SELECTED SHORT STORIES, D. H. Lawrence. 128pp. 0-486-27794-1
THE CALL OF THE WILD, Jack London. 64pp. 0-486-26472-6
FIVE GREAT SHORT STORIES, Jack London. 96pp. 0-486-27063-7
THE SEA-WOLF, Jack London. 248pp. 0-486-41108-7
WHITE FANG, Jack London. 160pp. 0-486-26968-X
DEATH IN VENICE, Thomas Mann. 96pp. (Available in U.S. only.) 0-486-28714-9
THE NECKLACE AND OTHER SHORT STORIES, Guy de Maupassant. 128pp. 0-486-27064-5
BARTLEBY AND BENITO CERENO, Herman Melville. 112pp. 0-486-26473-4
THE OIL JAR AND OTHER STORIES, Luigi Pirandello. 96pp. 0-486-28459-X
THE GOLD-BUG AND OTHER TALES, Edgar Allan Poe. 128pp. 0-486-26875-6
TALES OF TERROR AND DETECTION, Edgar Allan Poe. 96pp. 0-486-28744-0

DOVER · THRIFT · EDITIONS

FICTION

THE QUEEN OF SPADES AND OTHER STORIES, Alexander Pushkin. 128pp. 0-486-28054-3

THE STORY OF AN AFRICAN FARM, Olive Schreiner. 256pp. 0-486-40165-0

FRANKENSTEIN, Mary Shelley. 176pp. 0-486-28211-2

THE JUNGLE, Upton Sinclair. 320pp. (Available in U.S. only.) 0-486-41923-1

THREE LIVES, Gertrude Stein. 176pp. (Available in U.S. only.) 0-486-28059-4

THE BODY SNATCHER AND OTHER TALES, Robert Louis Stevenson. 80pp. 0-486-41924-X

THE STRANGE CASE OF DR. JEKYLL AND MR. HYDE, Robert Louis Stevenson. 64pp. 0-486-26688-5

TREASURE ISLAND, Robert Louis Stevenson. 160pp. 0-486-27559-0

GULLIVER'S TRAVELS, Jonathan Swift. 240pp. 0-486-29273-8

THE KREUTZER SONATA AND OTHER SHORT STORIES, Leo Tolstoy. 144pp. 0-486-27805-0

THE WARDEN, Anthony Trollope. 176pp. 0-486-40076-X

FATHERS AND SONS, Ivan Turgenev. 176pp. 0-486-40073-5

ADVENTURES OF HUCKLEBERRY FINN, Mark Twain. 224pp. 0-486-28061-6

THE ADVENTURES OF TOM SAWYER, Mark Twain. 192pp. 0-486-40077-8

THE MYSTERIOUS STRANGER AND OTHER STORIES, Mark Twain. 128pp. 0-486-27069-6

HUMOROUS STORIES AND SKETCHES, Mark Twain. 80pp. 0-486-29279-7

AROUND THE WORLD IN EIGHTY DAYS, Jules Verne. 160pp. 0-486-41111-7

CANDIDE, Voltaire (François-Marie Arouet). 112pp. 0-486-26689-3

GREAT SHORT STORIES BY AMERICAN WOMEN, Candace Ward (ed.). 192pp. 0-486-28776-9

"THE COUNTRY OF THE BLIND" AND OTHER SCIENCE-FICTION STORIES, H. G. Wells. 160pp. (Not available in Europe or United Kingdom.) 0-486-29569-9

THE ISLAND OF DR. MOREAU, H. G. Wells. 112pp. (Not available in Europe or United Kingdom.) 0-486-29027-1

THE INVISIBLE MAN, H. G. Wells. 112pp. (Not available in Europe or United Kingdom.) 0-486-27071-8

THE TIME MACHINE, H. G. Wells. 80pp. (Not available in Europe or United Kingdom.) 0-486-28472-7

THE WAR OF THE WORLDS, H. G. Wells. 160pp. (Not available in Europe or United Kingdom.) 0-486-29506-0

ETHAN FROME, Edith Wharton. 96pp. 0-486-26690-7

SHORT STORIES, Edith Wharton. 128pp. 0-486-28235-X

THE AGE OF INNOCENCE, Edith Wharton. 288pp. 0-486-29803-5

THE PICTURE OF DORIAN GRAY, Oscar Wilde. 192pp. 0-486-27807-7

JACOB'S ROOM, Virginia Woolf. 144pp. (Not available in Europe or United Kingdom.) 0-486-40109-X